Edmond About

The Round of Wrong

Edmond About

The Round of Wrong

ISBN/EAN: 9783337348786

Printed in Europe, USA, Canada, Australia, Japan

Cover: Foto ©Andreas Hilbeck / pixelio.de

More available books at **www.hansebooks.com**

THE

ROUND OF WRONG

A Romance of To-Day

BY

EDMOND ABOUT

AUTHOR OF "THE GREEK BRIGAND, OR KING OF THE MOUNTAINS"
ETC.

Parlour Library Edition

LONDON

WARD, LOCK AND TYLER

WARWICK HOUSE, PATERNOSTER ROW

CONTENTS.

THE ROUND OF WRONG.

CHAPTER I.

THE NEW YEAR'S GIFTS.

In the centre of the Rue de l'Université, in Paris, there are four mansions, which may be reckoned as among the handsomest even in that city of palaces. It is in one of these, belonging to the Baron de Sanglié, and joining the corner of the Rue de Bellechasse, that our story opens.

It is certainly a house of very stately aspect. The gate opens on a courtyard covered with the finest sand, and surrounded by evergreens. The porter's lodge is to the left, hidden beneath a thick trellis of ivy, where the sparrows and the porter try to outvie each other in gossiping. The ground and first floors of the mansion are occupied by the Baron himself; they look out on a large garden peopled by tom-tits, blackbirds, and squirrels, which visit each other at perfect ease, just as if they were the denizens of a wood, and not citizens of Paris.

The arms of the Sanglié family are painted on the panels along the Hall. They consist of a Boar, *or*, on a

B

field *gules.* The shield is supported by two greyhounds, while underneath runs the motto, SANG LIÉ
AU ROI.*

Half-a-dozen living greyhounds, grouped according
to their fancy, are biting at the veronicas blossoming
in china vases, or lying on the matting, with their
snake-like heads resting on their paws. The footmen,
lounging about on the benches, have their arms
solemnly crossed, as befits people attached to a noble
family.

On the 1st of January, 1853, at about nine in the
morning, all the servants of the house were holding a
noisy congress in the hall, for the Baron's steward, M.
Anatole, had just given them their New Year's Gifts.†
The head cook received twenty pounds, the valet ten
pounds. Even the least favoured of all, the scullery-
boy, looked with inexpressible tenderness on two bran
new Louis-d'or. There might be jealousy among
them, but no dissatisfaction, and each said in his own
peculiar language that it was a pleasure to serve a
master at once so rich and so generous.

These gentry formed rather a picturesque group
round the stove. The earliest risers among them
were dressed in full livery, while others still wore the
sleeved waistcoat, or undress uniform of servants. The

* "Blood allied to the King." It is a pun on the word
"Sanglier," or boar, which cannot be rendered in English.
Hence we pray our readers to pardon the enforced Gallicism.

† In France it is the custom for everybody to give everybody
presents on New Year's-day, and servants look for a species of
bounty, varying in amount with the position of the family they
serve, and their own status in the domestic hierarchy.

THE NEW YEAR'S GIFTS. 3

valet was dressed all in black, with list slippers; the
gardener resembled a villager in his Sunday clothes;
the coachman had on a striped waistcoat, and his gold-
bound three-cornered hat; while the porter wore his
golden aiguillettes and wooden shoes.

As the master usually slept till mid-day, after
spending the night at his club, there was plenty of
time for them to go to work. Each was spending his
money beforehand, and the castles in the air had
reached the seventh story. After all, every man,
great or small, has some of the Alnaschar blood in
his veins.

"With that, and what I have already saved," the
steward said, "I shall have a very tidy annuity.
Thank Heaven! there is bread on the shelf, and I shall
not want for anything in my old days."

"Hang it," the valet remarked, "you're a bachelor,
and have only yourself to think of. But I've got a
family. So I'll give my money to a young man I
know on the Stock Exchange, and he'll turn it over
well."

"That's a good idea, Mr. Ferdinand," the scullery-
boy said, "so pray take my forty francs too, when
you go."

The valet replied in a protecting tone, "How green
he is! What can be done with forty francs on the
Exchange?"

"Well, then," the young man said, stifling a sigh,
"I will place them in the savings-bank."

The coachman uttered a loud laugh, and struck his
stomach as he said, "That's my savings-bank. I

B 2

always put my money there, and never was the worse
for it.   Don't you think so, Master Altroff?"

Altroff, porter by profession, Alsacian by birth—
tall, vigorous, bony, with wide shoulders and enormous
head, and as rubicund as a young hippopotamus, per-
petrated a wink and gave a "cl'c" with his tongue
worth a long phrase.

The gardener, a true Norman, fingered the money
in his hand, and remarked, "Ah! bah! money drunk
is money sunk.   There is no investment like a hiding-
place in an old wall or a hollow tree.   Hide your
pelf, you'll enjoy it yourself.   He who lends, loses his
friends.   Money in your purse, let the old one do his
worst."

All present protested against such simplicity as
burying money instead of letting it turn over.   Some
twenty exclamations were heard simultaneously.   Each
revealed his secret, and betrayed his weakness.   Each
tapped his pocket and enjoyed his certain hopes—the
clear and liquid happiness he had pouched that morning.
Gold mingled its shrill weak voice with their conceited,
vulgar passions, and the clinking of the Napoleons,
more heady than the odour of wine, or the smell of
gunpowder, turned their poor brains and heightened
the beating of their coarse hearts.

At the height of the tumult a small door opened on
the staircase, about half way up.   A woman dressed
in black rags, came down the steps hurriedly, crossed
the hall, opened the glass door, and disappeared in the
court-yard.

It was the affair of a moment; yet this gloomy apparition destroyed all the happiness of the servants. They rose as she passed with marks of profound respect. The shouts were arrested in their throats. The gold no longer rang in their pockets. The poor woman left behind, as it were, an exhalation of silence and stupor. The valet, as a strong-minded man, was the first to recover.

"Confuse it," said he, " I really fancied I saw Misery in person pass. My New Year's day is spoiled. You'll see that I shall succeed in nothing till next New Year's Eve. Bru! I'm cold all up the back."

" Poor woman !" the steward said ; " she has had her thousands and her hundreds, and now see ! Who'd believe she was a duchess ?"

" Her rogue of a husband spent it all."

" A gambler !"

" A glutton !"

" An old scamp, who runs after all the petticoats from morning till night."

" I don't feel any sympathy with him ; he's only got his deserts."

" Does any one know how little Germaine is ?"

" Their negress told me she is at the last stage. She spits blood by the handkerchief-full."

" And hasn't even a carpet in her room. That poor child could only recover in a warm country—at Florence, or in Italy."

" She'll become an angel in heaven."

" Those who remain behind are most to be pitied."

" I don't know how the Duchess can get on much longer. They've run up bills with every tradesman, and the baker is talking of stopping their credit."

" What's their rent ?"

" Eight hundred francs. But I should be surprised if master ever saw the colour of their money."

" If I were he, I would sooner have the rooms empty than keep people who disgrace the house."

" What an ass you are ! I suppose the Duke de la Tour and his family are to go to the workhouse.—No, no ; we have all an interest in keeping the matter from becoming public."

" But why don't they work ?" the scullery-boy said. " Dukes are men like others."

" Boy," the steward said, seriously, " we are talking of things you do not understand. The proof that they are not like other men is, that I, your superior, shall never be a baron, even for an hour, in my life. Besides, the Duchess is a glorious lady, and does things of which neither you nor I would be capable. Would you like to eat stewed beef for every meal through the year ?"

" Hang it, stewed beef ain't particularly jolly !"

" Well ! the Duchess only puts the pot on to stew every other day, because her husband is not fond of broth. He has a rich tapioca soup, a beefsteak, or a couple of chops for his dinner, while the poor dear lady eats the shreds of meat of which the soup was made. What do you say to that ?"

The scullery-boy was touched to the heart,—" My good M. Tournoy," he said to the steward, " they are really interesting people ; could we not send them something nice, by coming to an understanding with their negress ?"

"Oh, no, she is as proud as they are; she wouldn't have anything to do with us, and yet it's my belief she don't breakfast every day."

This conversation would have lasted longer, had not M. Anatole come to interrupt it; he arrived just at the moment to stop the porter, who was opening his mouth for the first time. The meeting dispersed with all speed; each orator carried off the implements of work, and the hall was deserted.

In the meanwhile, Marguerite de Brisson, Duchess de la Tour d'Embleuse, was walking with hasty steps in the direction of the Rue Jacob. The passers by, who elbowed her as they hastened to give or receive their New Year's gifts, found her like those wretched Irish girls who wander about the streets of London in search of a penny. Daughter of the Duke of Brittany, wife of an ex-governor of Senegal, the Duchess wore a black straw bonnet, the edge of which was in rags; her veil was torn in five or six places, and hardly concealed her face. An old China crape shawl, rusty and weather-worn, hung from her shoulders, the ragged fringe trailing in the snow; the dress under it was so worn that the material could not be recognised; it would have required a very close examination to see that it was a moire unmoired, muddy, cut in the folds, worn out at the bottom, and corroded by the mud of Paris streets. No linen was to be seen at the neck or cuffs. As she crossed a gutter, she would lift her dress, and you might observe a grey worsted stocking, and a plain black mohair petticoat. The Duchess' hands, stung by the piercing cold, were concealed in her shawl, and she dragged her feet after her as she walked—not from any bad habit, but simply through fear of losing her slippers.

And yet by a contrast you may have noticed sometimes, the Duchess was neither thin nor pale, nor in any way disfigured by wretchedness. She had received from her ancestors one of those rebellious beauties which resist everything—even hunger. Prisoners have been known before now to grow fat in their dungeons to the day of their death. At the age of forty-seven the Duchess retained the greater portion of her beauty. Her hair was black, and she had two-and-thirty teeth, strong enough to pound the hardest crust. Her health was less flourishing than her face, but that was a secret between herself and her physician. The Duchess was approaching a dangerous period of life, and had received several serious warnings. Dr. le Bris, a young physician and old friend, recommended a gentle course of life, without fatigue or emotion. But how could she endure such harsh trials without giving way to emotions?

Duke Cæsar de la Tour d'Embleuse, son of one of the émigrés most faithful to the king, and most vindictive against his country, was magnificently rewarded for his father's services. In 1827, Charles X. appointed him Governor-General of the French possessions in Western Africa. He was hardly forty years of age. During his eighteen months' stay in the colony he made head against the Moors and the yellow fever, and then requested leave to come to Paris to be married. He was rich, thanks to the indemnity, and he doubled his fortune by marrying the lovely Marguerite de Brisson, who had an estate bringing in two thousand five hundred pounds a-year. The King signed his marriage contract on the same day as the Ordinances, and the Duke saw himself married, and discharged from office at one blow. The new Power would gladly have welcomed him among the turncoats, and it was rumoured that Louis Philippe's Ministry made some advances to him. But he despised all offices, in the first place, through pride, and then, through his invincible sloth. Whether it was that he had expended in three years his entire stock of energy, or that the facile loves of Paris held him by an irresistible attraction, his only labour, during ten years, was parading his horses in the Park, and showing his yellow kid gloves at the opera. Paris had been hitherto a *terra incognita* to him, for he had lived in the country under the inflexible ferule of his father until the day that he started for Senegal. He enjoyed every pleasure so late in life that he had no time to outgrow many of them.

All pleased him—the enjoyments of the table—the satisfaction of his vanity—the emotions of gambling, and even the placid joys of domestic life. He displayed at home the attentions of a young husband ; and abroad the impetuosity of a youth just of age. His wife was the happiest in France, but she was not the only woman whose happiness he promoted. He wept tears of joy on the birth of his daughter in the summer

of 1835. In the excess of his delight he bought a
country villa for an opera dancer with whom he was
madly in love. The dinners he gave at home were
unrivalled, save by the suppers he gave at his mistress'
The world, which is always indulgent to men, pardoned
him for thus squandering his life and his fortune. He
was considered to act as a gentleman, because his
pleasures abroad awoke no painful echo at home.
Looking at it in the right light, ought he to be re-
·proached for spreading around him the superabundance
of his purse and his heart? Not a woman pitied the
Duchess, and, in fact, there was no reason to pity her.
He carefully avoided compromising himself; he never
appeared in public with any lady but his wife, and
would sooner have missed a rendezvous than allow her
to go to a ball by herself.

This double life, and the decent veil a gentleman
always seeks to throw around his pleasures, soon en-
croached on his capital. Nothing costs so much at
Paris as obscurity and discretion. The Duke was too
great a gentleman to bargain with anybody; he could
never refuse anything to his own, or another person's
wife. You must not suppose that he was ignorant
of the enormous breaches he was making in his fortune;
but he calculated on play to repair them all. Men to
whom fortune has come in their sleep, accustom themselves to place unlimited confidence in destiny. The
Duke was as lucky as every man who takes to cards
for the first time. It was supposed that his gains in
1841 more than doubled his income. But nothing is
permanent in this world, not even luck in play, and he

speedily discovered this fact. The Revolution of 1848, which exposed so much misery, taught him that he was irretrievably ruined. He saw a bottomless abyss yawning before him, but where another man would have lost his senses, he did not even lose hope : he went straight to his wife, and said, gaily, " My dear Marguerite, this unlucky revolution has stripped us of everything. We have not fifty pounds left."

The Duchess did not expect such a piece of news ; she thought of her daughter, and wept bitterly.

" Do not be afraid," he said ; " it is only a passing storm. Trust to me, and trust to accident. People say I am a light-minded man : all the better—I shall not sink."

The poor lady wiped away her tears, and said to him,—

" I suppose, my love, you will take office ?"

" I—fie ! I will await Fortune ; she is a coquette, but she is too fond of me to think of leaving me without some intention of returning."

The Duke waited for her coming eight years in a small set of rooms, over the stables at the Baron de Sanglié's. His old friends, so soon as they had time to look round, helped him with their purses and their credit. He borrowed without scruple, like a man who had lent much without any acknowledgment. He was offered several appointments, all honourable ; an agricultural company proposed to place him on the direction with a handsome salary. He refused through fear of lowering himself : "I do not mind selling my time," he said, " but I cannot consent to lend my name."

Thus he descended, one by one, all the rungs of misery's ladder, wearing out his friends, exhausting the patience of his creditors, causing every door to be closed against him, staining the honour he would not compromise, but never thinking of the threadbare coat in which he promenaded the streets, or the fireless grate at home.

On the first of January, 1853, the Duchess was carrying to the government pawnbroker's her wedding-ring.

A person must be totally destitute of all human help to pledge an article of such slight value as a wedding-ring. But the Duchess had not a farthing in the house; and it is not possible to live without money, although confidence is the mainspring of commerce in Paris. Many things may be obtained without payment if you can throw on the counter a card bearing a high name and an imposing address. You can furnish your house, fill your cellar, and cram your wardrobe without letting your tradespeople see the colour of your money. But there are a thousand daily expenses which can only be defrayed purse in hand. A coat may be got on credit, but mending a rent costs ready-money. It is at times easier to buy a watch than a cabbage. The Duchess had a remnant of credit with some tradespeople, which she managed with religious care; but as for money, she knew not where to turn for it. The Duke had no friends left: he had expended them like the remains of his fortune. One college friend is fond of us up to fifty pounds; an acquaintance may be the man to lend us a twenty-pound note; or a charitable neighbour may represent the value of a dinner. Beyond a certain figure, the lender is liberated from all the duties of friendship ;— he has no reason to reproach himself ; he has behaved well ; he owes you nothing more, and has the right to turn his head away when he meets you, or to be " not at home" when you call. The Duchess' lady-friends had withdrawn from her one by one. The friendship of women is assuredly more chivalrous than that of men ; but in both sexes affection is only last-ing among equals. A delicate pleasure is felt in climbing a difficult flight of stairs two or three times, and sitting down in full-dress by the side of a truckle-bed ; but there are few souls sufficiently heroic to live on familiar terms with the misfortunes of others. The poor woman's dearest friends, those who addressed her by her Christian name, felt their hearts chilled in this room, without carpet or fire—but they did not come again. When the Duchess' name was mentioned, they spoke highly of her, sincerely pitied her, and said, " We still love her dearly, but we hardly ever see her. It is her husband's fault."

In this lamentable state of desertion, the Duchess had recourse to the last friend of the wretched—the creditor who lends at high interest, but without reproach or objection. The pawnbroker took care of her jewellery, furs, and the best of her linen and wardrobe, and the last mattrass on her bed. She had pledged everything under the eyes of the old Duke, who saw article after article of his furniture disappear, and gaily wished them a pleasant trip. This incom-prehensible old man lived in his house, as Louis XIV did in his kingdom, without care for the future, while saying, " After me, the deluge !" He rose late, break-fasted with a good appetite : passed an hour at his toilet-table, curled his hair, plastered his wrinkles, put on some rouge, polished his nails, and promenaded his graces about Paris until the dinner hour. He did not feel surprised at seeing a good meal on the table, and was too discreet to ask his wife whence she obtained it. If the fare were meagre, he only smiled at his ill-luck. When Germaine began coughing, he made some agree-able jokes about this bad habit. He was a long time before he saw that she was pining away ; and on the day he perceived it, he experienced considerable annoy-ance.

When the doctor told him that the poor girl could only be saved by a miracle, he called him Dr. Croaker, and said, as he rubbed his hands, " Pooh, pooh ! it will be nothing !" He did not really know whether he assumed this jaunty air to reassure his family, or if his natural levity prevented him from experiencing grief. His wife and daughter adored him, such as he was. He treated the Duchess with the same attention as on the day after their marriage, and jumped Germaine on his knee. The Duchess never suspected that he had been the cause of her ruin ; she had seen in him, for three-and-twenty years, a perfect man ; she considered his indifference to be courage and firmness ; she hoped in him, spite of all, and believed him capa-ble of raising her family again by a stroke of fortune.

According to Dr. Le Bris' opinion, Germaine had still four months to live. She would die at the be-

ginning of spring, and the white lilies would have time
to blossom over her tomb. She foresaw her fate, and .
judged of her condition with a degree of clairvoyance
very rare among consumptive persons. Perhaps, too,
she suspected the evil that was undermining her mother's
health. She slept by the side of the Duchess, and in
her long nights of watchfulness she was at times
alarmed by the panting sleep of her dear nurse. "When
I am dead," she thought, "mamma will soon follow
me; we shall not be separated for long—but what will
become of papa?"

Every possible anxiety, privation, physical and moral
pain, inhabited this nook of Sanglié House; and in
Paris, so pregnant with wretchedness, there was not,
probably, a family more thoroughly wretched than that
of the La Tour d'Emblcuse's, whose last resource was a
wedding-ring.

The Duchess first hurried to a branch pawnbroker's
office, but found it closed, for was it not a holiday?
Then she tried another—also closed! Her resources
were exhausted, for there are few such establishments
in an aristocratic quarter like St. Germain. Still, as
the Duke could not begin the year by fasting, she went
into a small jeweller's shop, where she sold her ring
for eleven francs. The tradesman promised to keep
it for three months, in case she would like to re-pur-
chase it.

She tied up the money in the corner of her handkerchief, and walked without stopping, to the Rue des
Lombards. She went into a chemist's, bought a bottle
of cod-liver oil for Germaine, crossed the market, pur-

chased a lobster and a partridge, and returned, muddy up to her knees, to her apartments.

She found in the ante-chamber her only servant, old Semiramis, weeping silently over a piece of paper.

"What have you there?" she asked her.

"It is all, madam, the baker has brought us; we cannot have any more bread unless we pay him."

The Duchess took the bill; it amounted to twenty-four pounds. "Don't cry," she said, "here is some change, and run to the nearest baker's; you will get a roll for your master, and some household bread for us. Carry that into the kitchen, it is your master's breakfast. Is your young mistress awake yet?"

"Yes, m'm. The doctor saw her at ten o'clock; he is still in master's room."

Semiramis went out, and the Duchess proceeded to her husband's room. On opening the door, she heard the duke saying, in a clear and resonant voice—

"Two thousand a year! I knew that luck was changing!"

CHAPTER II.

DR. CHARLES LE BRIS is one of the men most liked in Paris. The great city has its spoiled children in every art, but I do not know one she treats with greater tenderness. He was born at a pretty little town in Champagne, but he studied at the Henri IV College. One of his relations, who is a surgeon in the country, destined him from an early hour for the profession. The young man walked the hospitals—passed his examination, and gained certain medals, which arc the ornament of his study. His sole ambition was to succeed his uncle, and finish the patients the good old gentleman had begun. But when he appeared, armed with his successes, and doctor to the teeth, the health inspectors of the town, and his uncle, who was not much better than they, asked him why he had not remained in Paris. He was so good-looking and so clever that they felt sure success awaited him there His venerable relation considered himself much too young to think of retiring, and the rivalry of his nephew restored him his long-lost legs. In short the poor fellow was so badly received, and so many obstacles were placed in his path, that in his despair he returned to Paris. His old masters had such a high

C

opinion of him that they soon got him a practice. Great men are rich enough not to be jealous. Thanks to their generosity, the doctor's reputation was made in five or six years. Some people like him as a clever man, others as an excellent dancer ; but all because he is a gentleman. He is ignorant of the first principles of charlatanism—speaks very little of his success, and leaves to his patients the care of stating who has cured them. He lives in a most unfashionable part of the town, on the third floor ; but the poor people in his quarter have no reason to complain of his being among them ; for he attends to them with so much application that he sometimes forgets his purse at their bedside.

M. le Bris had been for more than three years Mademoiselle de la Tour's physician. He had watched the progress of the disease without being able to do anything to check it. It was not that Germaine was one of those children condemned at their birth, who have within them the germ of an hereditary death. Her constitution was robust—her chest wide, and her mother had never coughed. A neglected cold, a freezing room, and want of actual necessaries had caused the whole evil. Gradually, in spite of the doctor's attention, the poor girl had grown pallid as a statue of wax ; her appetite, gaiety, breath, and delight in life, all failed her. Six months before this history begins, M. le Bris had called in two celebrated physicians to her ; they gave their opinion that she could still be saved. One lung was left her, and nature is contented with that. But she must be taken without delay to Egypt or Italy.

"Yes," the young doctor said, "the only prescription is a villa on the banks of the Arno, a quiet life, and an income. But look!"

He pointed to the torn curtains, the straw chairs, and the naked floor.

"These condemn her to death."

In the month of January the other lung was attacked : the sacrifice was being consummated. The doctor transferred his care to the Duchess, and his last hope was to lull the daughter gently to sleep and save the mother.

He paid his visit to Germaine, felt her pulse as a matter of form, offered her a box of sugar-plums, kissed her fraternally on the forehead, and went into the Duke's room.

The Duke was still in bed; his face was not made up, and he showed all his three-and-sixty years.

"Well, my good doctor," he said, with a hearty laugh, "what sort of a year do you bring us? Is Fortune still angry with me? Ah, you coquette. If ever I get hold of you! You are witness, doctor, that I am waiting for her in bed."

"My lord Duke," the doctor replied, "as we are alone, we can talk on serious matters. I have not concealed from you your daughter's state."

The Duke gave a little sentimental pout, and said,

"Really, doctor, is there no hope left? Come, do not indulge in false modesty; you are capable of a miracle."

M. le Bris shook his head sadly. "All that is in my power," he replied, "is to assuage her sufferings."

c 2

"Poor little one. Just imagine, my dear doctor, that she wakes me up every night with her coughing. She must suffer fearfully, though she denies it. If there is no hope left, her last hour will be a mercy."

"That is not all I had to say to you; still, pray pardon me if I begin the year with evil tidings."

The Duke sat up in bed. "What is it? you alarm me."

"The Duchess has caused me great anxiety for the last few months."

"Now, really, doctor, you are trying your evil omens again. The Duchess, thank Heaven, is in good health —I only wish I was as well."

The doctor entered into certain details which shook the old man's frivolity tremendously. He fancied himself alone in the world, and he was seized with a fit of shuddering. His voice was lowered a tone, and he clung to the doctor's hand as the drowning man does to the last branch. "My dear friend," he said to him, "save me! I mean, save the Duchess! I have only her left in the world. What would become of me? She is an angel—my guardian angel. Tell me what I must do to save her, and I will obey you like a slave."

"My lord Duke, the Duchess requires a calm and easy life, free from emotions and special privations; a careful dietary, nourishing food, a comfortable house, and a carriage."

"And the moon, I suppose!" the Duke exclaimed, impatiently. "I thought you had more sense, doctor, and better eyesight. Carriage, house, good food!

Go and find them for me, if you wish me to give them to her."

The doctor replied without the slightest trace of irritation : " I bring them to you, your Grace, and you have only to take them."

The old man's eyes sparkled like those of a cat suddenly going into a dark room. " Speak," he shouted ; "you are torturing me alive."

" Before telling you anything, I think it necessary to remind you that I have been the nearest friend of your family for the last three years."

" You may say the only one ; nobody will contradict you."

" The honour of your name is as dear to me as to yourself, and if—"

"That will do ; that will do !"

" Do not forget that the life of the Duchess is in danger ; that I promise to save her, provided that you supply me with the money."

" Hang it all ! you must find it for me : to the point, doctor, to the point."

"I have come to it. Have you ever met in Paris the Count de Villanera ?"

" The black horses ?"

" Exactly."

" The handsomest turn-out in Paris."

" Don Diego Gomez de Villanera is the last scion of a great Neapolitan family that was transplanted to Spain in the reign of Charles I. His fortune is the largest in the whole Peninsula. If he cultivated his estates, and worked his mines, he would have at least

a hundred thousand pounds a-year.   As it is, he has
half that amount : he is thirty-two years of age, is good-
looking, perfectly educated, possesses a most honourable
character—"

"You can add—and Madame Chermidy."

"As you are aware of that fact, I can shorten my
story.   The Count, for reasons too long to explain here,
wishes to leave Madame Chermidy, and marry into one
of the most illustrious families in Paris.   So little does
he seek fortune, that he will settle on his father-in-law
two thousand pounds a year.   The father-in-law he
desires is yourself; and he has charged me to find out
your views.   If you assent, he will come this very day
to ask your daughter's hand, and the marriage ceremony
will be performed in a fortnight."

The Duke bounded to the foot of the bed, and looked
the doctor fixedly in the face.

"You are not mad?" he said, "you are not playing
with me?   You cannot forget that I am the Duke de
la Tour, and twice your age?   Are you really speaking
the truth?"

"On my honour !"

"But he does not know that Germaine is ill?"

"He knows it."

"Dying?"

"Yes !"

"Given up?"

"He knows that, too."

A cloud passed across the old Duke's face.   He sat
down by the side of the empty fireplace, not noticing
he was almost naked.   He leant his elbows on his knees,
and pressed his head between his hands.

"It is not natural!" he went on. "You have not told me all; and the Count must have some seeret motive for asking the hand of a girl who may be regarded as dead."

"It is true," said the doctor; "but pray return to your bed. I have a long story to tell you."

The Duke returned to his blankets. His teeth rattled with cold and impatience, and he fixed his eyes on the doctor with the restless curiosity of a child watching a box of sugarplums being opened. M. le Bris did not keep him waiting long.

"You are aware," he said, "of his position with Madame Chermidy?"

"The easily consoled widow of a husband who was never seen."

"I met Monsieur Chermidy three years back, and can guarantee that his wife is not a widow."

"All the better for him! hang it! husband of Madame Chermidy; that's a sinecure which must produce a handsome income."

"How easily rash judgments are formed! Monsieur Chermidy is an honourable man, and an officer, indeed, of some distinction; I do not think he comes from any high family; at the age of thirty-three, he was still captain of a West India trader. He entered the Royal Navy as quartermaster, and in two years obtained his commission as officer. In 1830 he laid his heart and his epaulette at the foot of Honorine Lavinaze;—all her fortune consisted in her fine eyes, her eighteen years, a showy little cap, and an unbounded ambition. She was not nearly so good looking as she is at present; —I know from her own lips that she was as dry as a

stick and as black as a young daw; but she was open
to public view and universally admired; she was in a
tobacconist's shop; and from the port-admiral down to
the youngest middy, the whole naval aristocracy of
Toulon came to smoke and sigh round her. But nothing could turn her strong head—neither the incense
of flattery nor the smoke of the cigars. She had taken a
vow to resist temptation until she had found a husband
—and no seduction availed. The officers christened
her the 'Cracker,' on account of her hardness; while
the townspeople called her 'Ulloa,' because she was
besieged by the French navy.

"There was no lack of honest offers—any quantity
of them are to be found in a seaport. On returning
from a lengthened cruise, a young officer has more illu-
sion, more simplicity and youth, than on the day of his
departure; the first woman that comes across him
appears to him as fair and holy as the France he has
returned to—it is his country in a silk gown. My good
fellow Chermidy, as simple as a round of beef, was
preferred for his candour, and he snatched up this coy
lamb from the teeth of his rivals.

"This piece of good fortune, which might have made
him enemies, in no way injured his prospects. Though
he lived retired with his wife in the country, he was
appointed to a ship without asking for it. From that
period he has only returned to France at lengthened
intervals; always at sea, he saved up his pay for his
wife, who, for her part, economized for him. Honorine,
improved by dress, by ease, and the filling up of angles,
was queen of the province for ten years. The only

events that signalized her reign were the bankruptcy
of a coal contractor, and the cashiering of two pay-
masters. In consequence of a disgraceful trial, in
which her name was not mentioned, she thought it
advisable to appear on a larger stage, and she took the
apartments she now occupies in Paris. Her husband
was steering for the banks of Newfoundland, while she
was coming up here. You were witness of her first
performance, I suppose ?"

"By Jove, yes ; and I'll venture to say that no
woman ever played her cards better. It is nothing to
be pretty and witty ; the great art consists in a woman
passing for a fortune, and then thousands are offered
her."

"She arrived here with some ten thousand pounds
raised from the Government offices. She made such a
dust in the city that you would have said the Queen of
Sheba had first landed in Paris. In less than a year
she made people talk of her horses, her dress, and her
furniture, while nothing positive could be said about
her behaviour. I attended on her for eighteen months
without getting hold of the right clue. I should have
gone on in my delusion had not her husband come
across me. He tumbled in upon her with his carpet
bag one day when I was visiting her. It was at the
beginning of 1850, three years back. The poor fellow
had just arrived from Newfoundland, and was going off
in a month for a five years' cruise on the China station,
and it was quite natural he should come and see his
wife between whiles. The livery of *his* servants made
his eyes twinkle : he was dazzled by the splendour of

his furniture. But, when he saw his dear Honorine appear in a morning costume which represented two or three years of his pay, he forgot to fall into her arms, tacked without saying a word, and started off for the Lyons station. In this way M. Chermidy let me into Madame's confidence, but I learned a good deal more from the Count de Villanera."

"Are we coming to the point ?" the Duke asked.

"A moment's patience. Madame Chermidy had noticed Don Diego some time before her husband's arrival. His box at the opera was next to hers, and she contrived to look at him in such a way that he procured an introduction to her. Any man you ask will tell you that her drawing-room is one of the most agreeable in Paris, though no other woman than the mistress of the house is met there. But she is a host in herself. The Count grew passionately attached to her, through the same spirit of rivalry which had ruined poor Chermidy. He loved her the more blindly because she seemed to yield to an irresistible fancy that forced her to give way. The cleverest man can be caught by such a bait, and there is no scepticism which can hold out against the force of real love. Don Diego is no simpleton. If he had guessed an interested motive, or surmised a calculated movement, he would have put himself on his guard, and all would have been lost. But the clever woman carried her skill to a degree of heroism. She exhausted all her resources, and spent her last shilling in persuading the Count that she loved him for himself alone. She even risked her reputation, of which she had taken such care, and would have madly compromised herself, had he not prevented it. His mother, a most respectable lady, sanctified by her age and stiffness, and like a picture of Velasquez just stepped from its frame, soon heard of her son's amour, and had nothing to say against it. She preferred to see him attached to a woman of the world than giving way to debasing excesses.

"The delicacy of Madame Chermidy was so ticklish, that Don Diego could never make her a present of the slightest thing. The first thing she accepted from him was the settlement of one thousand five hundred pounds a-year upon her. She was confined of a son in November, 1850. And now, my lord Duke, we have reached the heart of the question.

"Madame Chermidy was confined at a village near St. Germain, and I was present. Don Diego, ignorant of our laws, and believing that everything was permissible to persons of his condition, wished to recognise the child. The oldest son of the Villanera family bears the title of Marquis de los Montes de Hierro. I proved to him that his son must be called Chermidy, or have no name at all, and the commander had passed through Paris in January, just in time to save appearances. We consulted by the lady's bedside. She declared that her husband would certainly kill her if she tried to impose on him this legal paternity. The Count added that the Marquis de Hierro would never consent to sign himself Chermidy. In short I registered the infant by the name of Gomez, born of parents unknown.

"The young father, at once happy and unfortunate,

told the circumstances to the old countess. She desired
to see the child, and she has since brought it up in her
own house. He is now two years of age, in excellent
health, and bearing a decided resemblance to the
twenty-four generations of the Villaneras. Don Diego
adores his son, and is inconsolable at seeing in him only
a nameless child. Madame Chermidy is the woman to
overthrow mountains to assure her heir the name and
fortune of the Villaneras. But the person most to be
pitied is the poor dowager. She foresees that Don
Diego will never marry for fear of disinheriting his
beloved son ; he will sell the family estates to settle
the money on him, and of this great name and magnificent property not a trace will be found fifty years hence.

"In this extremity, Madame Chermidy has discovered a stroke of genius. 'Marry,' she said to her
lover ; 'seek a wife among the highest families of
France, and obtain that in the marriage contract she
recognise your child as hers. By this condition, little
Gomez will be your legitimate son, noble on both sides,
and heir of all your estates in Spain. Do not think of
me ; I am ready to sacrifice myself.'

"The Count submitted this scheme to his mother,
and she is delighted at it. She has lost her illusions
as to Madame Chermidy, who has cost Don Diego
something like one hundred and fifty thousand
pounds, and who talks of retiring to a hovel to
lament her past happiness while thinking of her
son ! M. de Villanera is the dupe of this false
resignation, and would fancy he was committing a crime
by abandoning this heroine of maternal love. At last

to satisfy his scruples, Madame whispered in his ears, 'Make a true marriage. The doctor will find you a wife among his patients.' I thought of your daughter, and have laid the matter before you, your Grace. This marriage, though it appears so strange at first sight, and though it gives you a grandson not of your blood, insures little Germaine a tranquil end, perhaps a prolonged existence; it saves the Duchess' life, and lastly——"

"It gives me two thousand pounds a-year, eh! doctor! Well, I am much obliged to you. You can tell the Count I am his obedient servant, but though my daughter is, perhaps to be buried, she is not for sale."

"My lord, it is true I offer you a bargain, but if I believed it unworthy a gentleman, believe me, I would not mix myself up with it."

"Hang it! doctor, every one regards honour in his own fashion. There is the soldier's honour, the tradesman's honour, and the honour of the gentleman, which will not allow me to become godfather of the little Chermidy. Two thousand pounds a year! Why, I had five thousand pounds, sir, without doing anything, either good or bad. I will not derogate from the traditions of my ancestry to gain such a sum as that."

"I would remind you, my lord Duke, that the Villanera family is worthy of an alliance with yours. The world could say nothing."

"Upon my soul, I really believe you will offer me presently a tradesman as son-in-law! I confess that, under any other circumstances, I should be well satisfied with Don Diego. He is of good birth, and I have

heard his family and person praised.   But, confound
it all, I should not like it to be said. 'Mdlle. de la
Tour had a son two years of age on the day of her
marriage.' "

"No one can say so, for nothing will be known.
The recognition will be secret, and suppose people
did talk of it?   Neither the law nor society makes any
distinction between a child legitimized and a legitimate
child."

"I fancy I see Germaine at the altar, with M. de
Villanera on her right hand, Madame Chermidy at his
left, a child of two years in her arms, and the old
scythe-bearer behind her.   Oh, it is simply abominable,
my poor doctor.   Do not talk about it further.   Is
the ceremony of recognition very complicated?"

"There is no ceremony at all.   A sentence in the
marriage contract, and all is settled."

"Ah! that is a sentence too many.   Drop the
subject.   You will promise not to say a word to the
Duchess?"

"I promise."

"Now, really, and is the poor Duchess so ill?   But
she runs about as if only fifteen."

"Her condition is very serious."

"And you believe, on your word, that **money** would
save her?"

"I would answer for her life, if I could obtain from
you—"

"You will obtain nothing at all.   I am true to my
race.   And you will allow there is some merit in my
refusal when I tell you I dare say we have not ten

pounds in the house. On my word as a gentleman, I really believe, if any one were to die here, we should not know where to get the money for the burial. All the worse! Nobility obliges! The Duke de la Tour does not take in little children to wean ; above all, not Madame Chermidy's child. I would sooner die in a workhouse. Doctor, I do not feel at all angry with you for tempting me. A man never knows himself thoroughly ; and I was not quite sure how I should look in presence of two thousand pounds a year. You have tried the pulse of my honour, and it is quite healthy. By the way, does the Count offer the principal, or merely the interest?"

"Whichever you please."

"And I have chosen poverty! Did I not tell you Fortune was a coquette? I have known her for a long period. We have been off and on with each other. Now she is making advances to me, but it will not do. Good-bye, doctor!"

The doctor rose, but the Duke still held him by the hand. "Do you not think I am performing an heroic action? You do not play?"

"I like a game at whist."

"Ah, then you are not a gambler! Learn, my friend, that if you once let the vein pass, it never returns. In refusing your offer, I renounce every prospect, I condemn myself to perpetual poverty."

"Accept, then, my lord Duke, and do not defy ill-fortune. What! I place in your hands the health of the Duchess, ease for yourself, a quiet and calm end for the poor girl, who is wasting away under privations

of every description ; I raise once more your family,
which was sinking in the dust. I give you a grandson
ready made, a magnificent child, who will ally your
name to that of his father—and what is the price of
all this ? A sentence of two lines inserted in a marriage
contract ; and you repulse me as the suggestor of a
disgraceful deed ! You would sooner condemn your
daughter, wife, and yourself, than lend your name to
a strange child ! You believe that you would sully
the memory of your ancestors ; but surely you know
at what price nobility was kept up in France, especially during the Crusades ? You must allow State
reasons ! How many names were saved by miracle or
skill ! How many genealogical trees revived by a
plebeian grafting !"

   " Why, nearly all, my dear doctor ; I could mention
twenty and not leave this street. Besides, an alliance
with the Villaneras is quite permissible ; the only
condition is that it should take place openly, without
hypocrisy. My daughter can recognise a stranger's
child to support the interests of two great French and
Spanish families. If any one ask why, we can reply,
for State reasons. And you will save the Duchess ?"

   " I pledge my word."

   " You will save my daughter, too ?"

   The doctor shook his head sadly. The old gentleman went on in a tone of resignation,—

   " Well, we cannot have everything. Poor child !
we would gladly have shared our comforts with her.
Two thousand pounds a year ! I knew that my luck
was returning."

The Duchess entered as these words were uttered, and her husband repeated to her the doctor's proposals with childish wonder. The doctor had risen to offer his chair to the poor lady, who had been running about without resting ever since she rose. She leant on the bed and listened with closed eyes to all that was said. The old gentleman, fickle as a man whose brain is not quite stable, had forgotten his own objections. He only saw one thing in the world, two thousand pounds a year. He was even so thoughtless as to tell the duchess of the dangers to which she was exposed, and that her life could only be saved in this way. But this revelation produced no effect on her.

She opened her eyes again, and turned them sorrowfully on the doctor.

"Then," she said, "Germaine is hopelessly condemned, as this woman wishes her lover to marry her."

The doctor tried to persuade her that all hope was not lost, but she stopped him by a sign, and said,—

"Do not disgrace yourself by a falsehood. These people have placed confidence in you; they have asked you to select a girl so ill, and in such a desperate state, that there is no fear of her recovery. If by any accident she were to live, and some day interposed between the two, to claim her rights, and expel the mistress, M. de Villanera would reproach you with having deceived him. You have run the risk of that."

M. le Bris could not help blushing, for the Duchess spoke the truth; but he escaped the danger by praising Don Diego. He painted him as a man of noble heart, a chevalier of the olden days. "Believe me, madame,"

D

he said to the Duchess, " that if our beloved patient
can be saved, she will be so by her husband. He
does not know her; has never seen her; he loves
another, and it is through a very sorrowful hope that
he decides to place a wife between himself and his
mistress. But the more interest he has to expect the
day of his widowhood, the more he will deem it his
duty to delay it. Not only will he surround his wife
with all the attentions her condition demands, but he
is capable of making himself her nurse, and watching
her night and day. I promise you that he will regard
marriage as seriously as all the other duties of life.
He is a Spaniard, and incapable of trifling with the
Sacraments; he adores his mother, and is passionately
fond of his child. Be assured that, from the day you
give him the hand of your daughter, he will have
nothing in common with Madame Chermidy. He will
take his wife to Italy; I shall accompany them, and
so will you, and if it please God to perform a miracle, we
shall be there to help."

"By Jove !" the Duke added, " everything is possible ; who would have told me this morning that I
should inherit two thousand a year ?"

At the word " inherit," the Duchess checked a flood
of tears just rising to her eyes.

"My love," she said, "it is a mournful thing when
parents inherit from their children. If it please God
to call to Him my poor Germaine, I shall bless His
rigorous hand in my tears, and await by your side
the moment that will re-unite us. But I wish that
the memory of my poor beloved angel shall be as pure

as her life. I have kept for more than twenty years an old bouquet of orange-flowers, faded like my happiness, my youth; I should like to be able to place them in her coffin."

"Ta! ta! ta!" the Duke exclaimed; "that is the way of women. You are ill, and orange-flowers will not cure you."

"As for me!" she said—her glance completed the sentence, and the Duke even understood it.

"That is it!" he said; "you will die together, I suppose. And pray, what will become of me?"

"You shall be rich, dear papa," Germaine said, as she opened the door of the sitting-room.

The Duchess rose with a bound, and ran to her daughter; but Germaine did not require any support; she kissed her mother and walked up to her father's bed with the firm and resolute step of a martyr.

She was dressed all in white. A sickly ray of the January sun fell on her face, and formed a sort of halo. Her face was colourless, and two large black eyes were the only signs of animation. A mass of golden hair, fine and curly, fell around her head. Beautiful hair is the last ornament of consumptive persons—they keep it to the end, and it is buried with them. Her transparent hands hung by her side, amid the folds of her dress. So thin was she, that she resembled one of those celestial creatures who possess none of the beauties or imperfections of woman.

She sat down familiarly on the bedside, passed one arm round her father's neck, held out her left hand to her mother, and gently drew her towards her.

Then she motioned M. le Bris to the chair, and said,—

"Sit down there, doctor, so that the family party may be complete. I do not repent having listened at the door. I was afraid I was not good for much, but your discussion has taught me I can do some little benefit here below. You are witnesses that I did not regret life, and went into mourning for it more than six months ago. This world is a very wretched residence for those who cannot breathe without suffering. My only regret was leaving my parents to a future of sorrow and want; but I am now calm. I will marry the Count de Villanera, and adopt that lady's child. Thanks to you, doctor, we are all saved. The misconduct of those persons will restore comfort to my dear father, and life to that sainted woman. I shall not die quite uselessly. All that was left me was the remembrance of a pure life, a simple unstained name, like the veil of a preparing nun. I surrender to my parents. Mamma, I must beg you not to shake your head; sick persons must not be thwarted—must they, doctor?"

"Germaine," he said, as he offered his hand, "you are an angel!"

"Yes; I am expected above; my niche is all ready. I will pray for you, my worthy friend, who never pray."

The Duchess shuddered as she listened to her; she feared lest her daughter's soul was about to take flight like a bird whose cage has been left open. She pressed Germaine to her breast, and said,—

"No, you shall not leave us! we will all go to

Italy, and the sun will cure you. M. de Villanera is
a generous man."

The patient shrugged her shoulders slightly, and
replied, "The gentleman of whom you speak would
do much better by remaining in Paris, where he finds
his pleasures, and leaving me to pay my debt quietly.
I know to what I pledge myself in assuming his name.
What would they say were I to play them the trick of
growing well? Madame Chermidy would appeal to
the laws to expel me from this world. Doctor, shall
I be obliged to see M. de Villanera?"

The doctor replied by a little affirmative sign.

"Well, then," she said, "I will receive him with a
pleasant face. As for the child, I shall be delighted
to see it, for I always loved children dearly."

The Duchess looked up to heaven, as a shipwrecked
man to the distant shore.

"If God is just," she said, "He will not separate
us; He will take us all together."

"No, dearest mamma, you will live for my father.
You, papa, will live for yourself."

"I promise it you," the old gentleman answered,
simply. Neither mother nor daughter suspected the
monstrous egotism concealed beneath this reply; they
were moved by it to tears, and the physician was the
only one who smiled.

Semiramis came to announce that the Duke's breakfast was on the table.

"Good-bye, ladies," said the doctor. "I am going
to carry the grand secret to the count. You will
possibly receive a visit from him this day.

"So soon?" the Duchess asked.

"We have no time to lose," said Germaine.

"In the meantime," the Duke interposed, "let us proceed to the most pressing matter. We will break-fast."

CHAPTER III.

THE WEDDING.

M. LE BRIS had a brougham at the door. He first drove to a large confectioner's, bought a sandal-wood box, which he ordered to be filled with sugar-plums, and then proceeded straight to Madame Chermidy. Although she had bought the house, she only occupied the first floor. The porter was in her service, and any visitor was announced by two strokes on a bell.

The doors opened of themselves before the young doctor. A footman took off his great coat with such skill that he hardly felt the wind of it, while another introduced him into the sitting-room. The count and Madame were at breakfast. The lady of the house offered him her cheek; while the count pressed his hand cordially.

The breakfast service was laid without a cloth on an oval table of sculptured oak. The walls were covered with old wood carving and modern pictures, while the ceiling was a copy of the " Banquet of the gods." The carpet came from Smyrna, the flower vases from Macao. A large Flemish candelabra, round panelled and thin armed, clung pitilessly to the ceiling, without respect for the assembled gods. Two sculptured sideboards displayed a profusion of silver plate and glass.

On the table the hot dishes and urn were silver, the plates old China, the bottles Bohemian, and glasses Venetian. The handles of the knives had once belonged to a China service in the possession of Louis XV

Had the doctor been fond of antitheses he might have made an interesting comparison between Madame Chermidy's furniture and Germaine's. But Parisian physicians are imperturbable philosophers who go from luxury to misery, without feeling the slightest surprise, just as they pass from heat to cold without even catching an influenza.

Madame Chermidy was wrapped up in a dressing-gown of white satin. In this dress she resembled a cat on an eider-down pillow, or a jewel in its case. You could imagine nothing more brilliant than her person, nothing softer than her covering. She was thirty-three years of age—the best age for women who have managed to take care of themselves. Beauty, the most perishable of earthly goods, is the most difficult to preserve. Nature gives it—art adds but little—only you must know how to keep it. Prodigal persons who squander it, and greedy persons who make no use of it, arrive in a few years at the same result. The woman of genius is she who governs herself with sensible economy. Madame Chermidy, who was born without passions and without virtues, sparing in her pleasures, ever perfectly calm, while affecting Southern vivacity, had taken as much care of her beauty as of her fortune. She nursed her freshness as much as a tenor does his voice. She was one of those women who will say foolish things at any moment,

but never do them, except at a good figure ; capable of
throwing a million out of window if it would bring in
two millions by the door—but too prudent to crack a
nut with her teeth. Her old admirers at Toulon
would hardly have known her, so much had she
changed to her advantage. Health mantled on her
cheek in small rosy clouds ; her small, round, plump
mouth was like a large cherry, which the sparrows
had pecked asunder ; her eyes sparkled like a fire made
of vine twigs ; her hair of a bluish-black, coming
down almost to her eyebrows, was parted on a pure
forehead, like the wings of a raven on the December
snow ; all about her was young, fresh, and smiling. It
would have indeed required good eyes to detect at
either corner of that pretty mouth, two almost imper-
ceptible wrinkles, fine as the hair of a newborn infant,
but which concealed an insatiable ambition, a will of
iron, a truly Chinese perseverance, and an energy
capable of every crime.

Her hands were perhaps rather short, but white as
ivory, with round, plump, pointed fingers. Her foot,
too, was like that of the Andalusian women, short
and rounded. She left it just as it was, and was not
so foolish as to wear long boots. All her little body
was plump and rounded, like her feet and hands ; her
waist rather thick — her arms a little fleshy — her
dimples a little too deep ; in short, she might be a
little too plump, but then it was the delicious plump-
ness of a quail, or the succulent roundness of a fine
pear.

Don Diego devoured her with his eyes in childish

admiration.   Are not lovers of all ages children?
According to the ancient Theogony, Cupid is a baby of
five years and a half, and yet Hesiod assures us that
he is older than time.

The Count de Villanera descends in a straight line
from the almost absurdly chivalrous Spaniards, whom
the divine Cervantes laughed at, though he could not
help admiring them a little.   Nothing about him revealed his Neapolitan origin, and it seemed as if his
ancestors had moved over with baggage and arms
among the old heroes of Spain.   He is a young,
thoughtful man, stiff, cold, rather haughty, but with
a heart of fire and a passionate soul.   He speaks but
little—never without reflecting, and he never told a
falsehood in his life.   He does not like discussion, and
hence does not converse gracefully.   He laughs very
rarely, but his smile is full of a certain affable grace
which is not without a degree of grandeur.   Gaiety, I
grant, would suit his face but badly.   Try to imagine
Don Quixote young, and in a black coat.   At the
first glance you notice his long-pointed, waxed, and
shining mustaches.   His long nose is curved like the
beak of an eagle : he has black eyes, eyebrows and
hair, and a complexion like an orange.   His teeth
would be fine were they not so long, and if he did not
smoke.   They are covered with a slight yellow coat-
,ng, but are so solid that mill-stones could be made of
them.   The white of his eye has also a yellow tinge,
still you cannot say that they are not fine eyes.   As
for his mouth, it is charming : you see, beneath his
mustaches, two lips as rosy as a child's.   His arms

and legs, his hands and feet have the aristocratic length. He is built like a grenadier, and has the manners of a prince.

If you now ask how a man so constituted could fall into the hands of Madame Chermidy, I will reply that the lady was more attractive and clever than Dulcinea of Toboso. People of Don Diego's stamp are not the most difficult to catch, and the lion rushes into the trap more rashly than the fox. Simplicity, rectitude, and all the generous impulses are so many defects in our armour. An honest heart does not easily suspect calculation and cunning of which it is itself incapable, and each makes the world according to his own image. If any one had told the count that Madame Chermidy loved him for interested motives, he would have shrugged his shoulders. She had asked him for nothing—he had offered her everything. In accepting the thousands she had done him a kindness—he was rather her debtor.

In the meanwhile, judging by the glances he turned upon her every now and then, it was easy to guess that the whole fortune of the Villaneras could change hands within a week. A dog, lying at its master's feet, is not more respectful or attentive than he was. In his large black eyes might be read that passionate gratitude, which every gentleman vows to the woman who has selected him, and the religious admiration of a young father for the woman who has borne him a child.

The little doctor, seated opposite the count, formed a singular contrast with him. M. le Bris is what is termed a pretty fellow. Perhaps he may be a trifle under the average height, but he is well made. His face is not stupid, but I never noticed what shape his nose was. He dresses with a neatness akin to elegance; his chestnut whiskers are carefully curled, and his hair is parted down his back. He is not a common-looking man by any means, but he does not rise beyond that category. No daughter to marry would refuse him for his appearance, but I should be much surprised if any woman drowned herself for him. He will take to stomach when he is forty years of age.

I know not any physician better suited for his round of patients. He pays visits from morning till night among all classes, and is at home everywhere. Women of every rank have worked zealously to make his reputation, and why? Because no matter whether the lady is old or young, pretty or ugly, he treats them all with equal politeness, with a tender gallantry—half composed of respect—half of love. He never entered into any explanation as to the nature of this feeling; perhaps he could not do so to himself. But all the women have a kind of compassion for him, which will carry him a long way.

His old hospital chums christened him from this reason, " The Key of Hearts." I know a house where he is called, and for good reasons, " The Tomb of Secrets."

" Well, 'Tomb of Secrets!'" Madame Chermidy said, in her slight Provençal accent, " have you found what I wanted?"

Yes, madame !"

"Is it the consumptive young lady you mentioned ?"

"Mlle. de la Tour."

"Good ! we are not lowering ourselves. I always took an interest in consumptive people. Women that cough ! So you see I am being rewarded for it."

"Doctor," the count asked, "did you mention the conditions ?"

"Yes, my dear count ; they are all accepted."

Madame Chermidy uttered a cry of joy. "Paris for me ! where duchesses are bought for ready money."

The count frowned, but the doctor said, quickly,—

"Had you been with me, madame, I know your heart so well that you would have wept."

"Is it then so touching, a duchess who sells her own daughter ? An episode of the slave-market ?"

"I would rather say an episode from the life of a martyr."

"You are polite to Don Diego !"

The doctor described the scene to which he had been witness. The count was moved. Madame Chermidy took out her handkerchief and wiped two pretty eyes which did not require it.

"I am much pleased," the count said, "that the resolution emanates from her. If the parents had accepted for her, I should, perhaps, have formed a bad opinion of them."

"Pardon me. Before judging them you ought to know if they had any bread in the house this morning."

"Bread !"

"Bread, without any metaphor !"

" Good-bye," said the count, " I will go and wish my mother a happy new year. She was asleep when I left the house this morning. I will tell her the result of your negotiations, and ask her what is to be done. What, doctor, there are really people in want of bread ?"

" I have met such persons during my life. Unfortunately I had not forty thousand pounds to offer them as I had to-day."

The count kissed Madame Chermidy's hand, and hastened to his mother's house. The pretty woman remained *tête-à-tête* with the doctor.

" As there are people who want bread," she said, " come, doctor, a cup of coffee ! How shall I have a chance of seeing this martyr to her chest ? For I must know to whom I am going to lend my child."

" Why, at church, say on the wedding-day."

" At church, she can go out then ?"

" Of course—in a carriage."

" I thought her more advanced than that."

" Did you want a marriage *in extremis ?*"

" No, but I wish to be quite sure. Good heavens, doctor, suppose that she were to get well ?"

" The faculty would be greatly surprised."

" And Don Diego would be really married, and I should kill you, Key of Hearts."

" Alas, madame, I do not feel in any danger."

" Why, alas ?"

" Pardon me, it was the physician who spoke and not the friend."

" When she is married you will still attend her ?"

" Must she be left to die without help ?"

" Why is the count going to marry her ? Not that she should live for ever, I suppose ?"

The doctor repressed a movement of disgust, and replied in the most natural tone, like a man in whom virtue is not pedantic,

" Really, madame, it is a custom I have, and I am too old to correct myself. We physicians attend to our patients as the Newfoundland dog pulls drowning persons from the water. It is an affair of pure instinct. A dog blindly saves his master's enemy, and I will take care of the poor creature as if we all felt an interest in saving her."

After the doctor's departure, Madame Chermidy proceeded to her dressing-room and gave herself into the hands of her tire-woman. For the first time for months she let herself be dressed without paying any attention to it : she had so many other cares. This marriage she had prepared—this skilful combination which she admired as a stroke of genius, might turn to her confusion and ruin. It only needed a caprice of nature or the stupid honesty of a physician to rout her most clever combinations, and cheat her dearest hopes. She began to doubt everything, her lover and her guiding star.

About three o'clock the visitors began defiling before her. She was obliged to smile on every pair of whiskers that approached her pretty face, and go into raptures over forty boxes of sugar-plums, which all came from the same shop. She heartily cursed the amiable vexations of New Year's day, but she allowed no trace of

the care that gnawed her to be seen.   All those who
left her sang her praises on the staircase.

She had a talent most precious for the lady of a
house : she knew how to make everybody talk.   She
spoke to each of what interested him most, she brought
people on to their own ground.   This woman of no
education, too idle and febrile to hold a book in her
hand, obtained a quantity of useful knowledge by
reading her friends.   They all thanked her most truly
for it.   We are all made so : in our hearts we thank
the person who compels us to utter our favourite
harangue, or tell the story we narrate best.   The person who enables us to show our wit is never a fool, and
when we are pleased with ourselves we cannot be dis-
pleased with anybody.   The most intelligent men
helped Madame Chermidy's reputation, some by supplying her with ideas, others by saying with secret
complacency, "She is a superior woman, for she understood me."

During the course of the afternoon she laid hands
on a celebrated homœopathist, who had one of the best
practices in Paris.   She found means to question him
before seven or eight persons on the point that weighed
so heavily on her mind.

"Doctor," she said, "you, who know everything, tell
me if consumptive people can be cured."

The homœopathist replied to her, that she would never
have to fear that disease.

"I am not talking of myself," she continued, "but
I am deeply interested in a poor girl whose lungs are
in a shocking state."

" Send me to her, madame ; no cure is impossible to homœopathy."

" You are very kind. But her physician, a simple allopath, assures me she has only one lung, and that is attacked."

" It can be cured."

" The lung, perhaps. But the patient ?"

" She can live with only one lung. It is a notorious fact. I do not promise that she will· be able to climb Mont Blanc, but she will live very comfortably for several years by means of care and globules."

" Why, you promise her miracles ! I did not think a person could live with only one lung."

" We have plenty of examples, as autopsy has proved."

" Autopsy—but that is only effected with the dead."

" You are right, madame, and I seem to be talking nonsense. Still, listen to this : In Algeria the cattle of the Arabs are generally consumptive. The herds are badly taken care of, pass the nights in the fields and catch lung diseases. Our Mussulman subjects do not call in the veterinary surgeon—they leave it to Mohammed to cure their cows and oxen. They lose a great number by this neglect, but do not lose them all. The animals recover sometimes without the help of art, and despite all the ravages the disease may have produced in their bodies. One of our army surgeons saw cows killed at Blidah quite cured of pulmonary consumption, and which had lived for several years with only one lung, and that in a very bad condition. Such is the autopsy I meant."

E

"I understand," Madame Chermidy said. "So, if all the people who live in our world were to be killed, we should find several who have not their whole allowance of lungs?"

"And who are not the worse for it. Precisely so, madame."

An hour later, Madame Chermidy saw an old hardened allopath come in, who did not believe in miracles, who was fond of putting things at the worst, and who was astonished that an animal so fragile as man could reach his sixtieth year without accident.

"Doctor," she said to him, "you ought to have come a little before ; you have lost a famous panegyric on homœopathy. M. P——, who has just left, boasted that he could make us all live with one lung. Would you have allowed him to say so ?"

The old physician raised his eyebrows.

"Madame," he replied, "the lungs are at once the most delicate and the most indispensable of all our organs ; they renew life at every second by a prodigy of combustion, which Spallanzani and the greatest physiologists have not explained or described. Their contexture is frightfully fragile ; their functions expose them to incessantly-recurring dangers. It is in the lungs that our blood comes into immediate contact with the external air. If we reflect that the air is always either too hot or too cold, or mingled with deleterious gases, we should never take a respiration till we had made our wills. A German philosopher, who had prolonged his life by prudence—the celebrated Kant, when he took his daily constitutional walk, was careful to keep his mouth shut, and breathe exclusively through his nostrils, so much did he fear the direct action of the surrounding atmosphere on the lungs."

"But in that case, my dear doctor, we are all condemned to die of our lungs."

"Most do die of them, madame, and the homœopathists will not alter it."

"But people are cured too. Suppose a young and healthy man marry a young but consumptive beauty. He takes her to Italy ; devotes himself to her cure, and gives her the assistance of men like yourself, would it not be possible in two or three years——?"

"To save the husband ? Possibly. But I would not promise it."

"The husband ! why, what danger can he run ?"

"The danger of contagion, madame. Who knows whether the tubercles that form in the lungs of a con·sumptive person do not spread in the surrounding atmosphere the seeds of death ? But pardon me, this is neither the time nor the place to develop a new theory, of which I am the inventor, and which I intend some of these days to lay before the Academy of Medicine. I will merely tell you a fact that came under my own observation."

"Pray tell us, my dear doctor ; it is a pleasure and a profit to listen to so learned a man as yourself."

"Five years ago I was attending the wife of a tailor —a poor little woman who was abominably consumptive. Her husband was a tall, stout, well-built German, as rosy as any apple. They adored each other. In 1849 they had a child that did not live, and in 1850

the wife died, though I had done all in my power to
save her. It was two years before I was called in
again, and then the tailor sent for me. I found him in
bed, so altered that I had some difficulty in recognising
him. He was in the third stage of consumption. I
saw a little woman crying by his bedside; he had been
foolish enough to marry again. He died, as I expected,
but his widow inherited the disease, and though I paid
her a visit yesterday, I cannot promise any certainty."

Madame Chermidy was "not at home" after five
o'clock, and indulged in a most melancholy meditation.
She had never despaired of becoming Countess Villanera. Every woman who deceives her husband
necessarily aspires to widowhood; the more so when
she has a rich and unmarried lover. She had every
reason to believe that Chermidy would not live for
ever. A man who passes his existence between sky
and water is a patient in danger of death.

Her hopes had assumed a solid shape since the birth
of little Gomez. She held the count by a tie omnipotent to honourable minds—paternal love. In marrying
the count to a dying woman she insured her son's future
and her own. But when on the point of accomplishing
this triumphant project, she discovered two dangers
she had not foreseen. Germaine might recover; or,
if she died, she might carry off the count with her, by
leaving him the germs of death. In the first case,
Madame Chermidy lost everything, even her child.
With what right could she reclaim the legitimated son
of Don Diego and Mlle. La Tour? On the other hand,
if the count must die after his wife, she did not feel

particularly anxious about marrying him. She felt
herself too handsome and too young to play the part of
the tailor's second wife.

" Fortunately," she thought, " there is nothing done
yet. Another expedient must be sought. The count is
in love, and a father. I can make him do everything
I please. If he must marry, in order to adopt his son,
we will find another person whose death is more sure
and malady not contagious." She consoled herself by
the thought that the allopath was an old original,
capable of inventing the most absurd theories. She
had heard it sustained, that consumption was, at times,
transmitted from father to son; but she found it natural
that Germaine could keep as her share the illness and
death. But what most seriously disturbed her was the
possibility of one of those marvellous cures which overthrow all the calculations of human prudence. She
began to hate Dr. le Bris, as much for his scruples as
his talent. Lastly, she determined on putting a
stopper on Don Diego's movements until she felt
quite sure.

But events had taken a great step during the day,
and the count came to tell her at ten in the evening
that her plans had been followed point for point.

Don Diego, on leaving her in the morning, hastened
to his mother. The old countess was a woman of the
same mould as her son—tall, wizened, bony, and
modelled like a plank, standing majestically on two
huge feet, black enough to frighten children, and
grinning an aristocratic smile between two bands of
grey hair. She listened to her son's report with that

stiff and disdainful condescension of the virtues of former times for the littlenesses of to-day. For his part, the count made no attempt to attenuate so much that was reprehensible in the calculations of his marriage.

These two honourable persons, forced by the pressure of circumstances into one of those scandalous bargains sometimes made in Paris, only thought of the means of doing a thing worthily which their ancestors would not have done at all. The dowager did not spice the conversation with any reproaches, even silent ones. The time for remonstrance had passed, and all that could be done now was to ensure the future of the family by saving the name of the Villaneras.

When everything was settled, the countess ordered her carriage and drove to Sauglié House. The baron's footman conducted her to the duchess's apartments. Semiramis opened the door and introduced her into the sitting-room. The duke and duchess received her near a small crackling fire, made of mysterious material : two planks from the kitchen, a straw-bottomed chair, and the wood of an old portmanteau. The duchess had dressed herself as well as she could; but her black velvet dress was blue at every seam. The duke wore the ribbon of his orders over a coat more threadbare than that of a writing-master.

The interview was cold and solemn. The duchess could not feel attracted to people who speculated on the speedy death of her daughter. The duke was more at his ease, and tried to be delightful. But the stiffness of the dowager-countess paralysed all his

graces, and he felt chilled to the marrow. The countess, through an error frequent enough at a first interview, formed a similar judgment of duke and duchess.
She suspected them of being anxious for the match,
and fancied she could read on their faces a sordid
joy : still she did not forget the pressing interests that
brought her here, and she coldly explained the reason
of her visit. She haggled like a lawyer, over all the
conditions of the marriage, and when both parties
were agreed on every point, she rose from her chair
and said, in a metallic voice :—

"My lord duke—my lady duchess—I have the
honour of asking you for the hand of Mlle. Germaine
de la Tour, your daughter, for Count Diego Gomez
de Villanera, my son."

The duke replied, that "his daugher was highly
honoured by being chosen by M. de Villanera."

The day for the marriage was agreed on, and the
duchess went to fetch Germaine to present her to
the dowager. The poor girl thought she must die of
terror, on appearing before this tall, spectral female.
The countess was pleased with her; spoke to her
maternally ; kissed her on the forehead, and said to
herself, "Why is she condemned to death? perhaps
she is a daughter-in-law that would suit me."

On returning home, the countess found Don Diego
playing with his son, in a room carpeted with toys.
The father and son formed a pleasant group, at which
a stranger would have smiled. The count handled the
frail creature with timid tenderness ; he trembled lest
a rash movement might tear his son piecemeal. The

boy was strong for his age; but ugly and shy to a degree. During the year he had been separated from his nurse, he had only seen two human beings—his father and grandmother—and lived between them, like Gulliver, in Brobdingnag. The dowager had withdrawn from society for his sake; she received and paid very few visits, for fear an imprudent word might betray the family secret. The only accomplices of this clandestine education were five or six old servants, who had grown grey in livery, people of another age and country. They looked like shipwrecked mariners, saved from the Invincible Armada. In the shadow of this strange family the child grew up sorrowfully. He had not the company of children of his own age, and it was lost labour to try and teach him to play. Some children of his age can speak fluently; he could scarce pronounce half a dozen words of two syllables. But Don Diego adored him; a father is always a father; but he was afraid of Don Diego. He called the old countess "mama," but seldom kissed her without crying. As for his mother, he knew her by sight; he saw her now and then in some remote spot, when visitors were rare. Madame Chermidy would leave her brougham in the distance, and come on foot to the count's carriage; she embraced the child by stealth; gave it sugar-plums, and said, with sincere tenderness, "My poor little boy, will you never be anything to me?" It would not have been prudent to take him to her house, even if the dowager had permitted it. All Paris suspected her position; but the world makes a great distinction between a woman convicted and a woman suspected.

Here and there were a few persons sufficiently simple to guarantee her virtue.

Madame de Villanera told her son that the request in marriage had been made and accepted. She praised Germaine, without saying anything of the family ; and described the misery in which they lived. Don Diego suggested a way of sending prompt assistance, without humiliating anybody. The countess wished simply to open her purse to the old duke, feeling quite convinced he would not refuse to dip into it, but the count considered it most decent to purchase the wedding present at once, and slip into one of the drawers a thousand pounds for the bride. These alms, concealed under flowers, would pay the pressing debts and support the family for a fortnight. No sooner said than done. The mother and son went out shopping ; but before going, the dowager kissed the tanned cheek of her grandson, saying, " Poor little bastard, you'll have a name as your New Year's gift."

Nothing is impossible in Paris ; so the corbeille was improvised in a few hours. All the tradespeople sent in during the evening, dresses, laces, cashmeres, and jewellery. The countess arranged it all herself, and placed the rouleaux of gold in the pin drawer. At ten o'clock the basket started for Sanglié house—the count to visit Madame Chermidy.

Germaine and the duchess spread out with cold curiosity the treasures sent to them. Germaine reminded her parents of that chapter in " Paul and Virginia" where she spends her aunt's money in little presents for her family and friends.

"What shall we do with all this?" she said, "now that we have no friends and no family. It is a large sum of money wasted."

The duke opened the drawers with noble disdain, like a man to whom all such splendour is a familiar object ; but his indifference gave way at the sight of gold : his eyes flashed ; his aristocratic hands, so often opened to give, greedily closed like the claws of a miser. He took a delight in opening all the rouleaux, and making the yellow gold sparkle in the light of a smoky lamp, he caused the coin to tinkle, which so joyously rang-in Germaine's funeral.

Passion is a brutal leveller, which equalizes all men. The duke could have played his part at nine that morning among the servants in the hall. Still, education gained the upper hand : the duke shut up the money in the drawer, and said, with well-feigned coldness,—

"It belongs to Germaine ; take care of it, my daughter. You will lend us a little, perhaps, to keep the pot boiling. Were I as rich as I shall be in a month, I would take you to sup at an eating-house, for our dinner was not very brilliant to-day."

The sick woman and the dying girl guessed the old man's secret covetousness. You cannot imagine with what tender earnestness, what respectful pity, Germaine forced some money upon him, and the duchess dressed him that he might go and sup in town. He returned about two in the morning; his wife and daughter heard an irregular step in the passage running past their door, but neither spoke, and each breathed regularly to make the other fancy she was asleep.

Don Diego and Madame Chermidy passed a stormy evening. The lady began by producing all her objections against the marriage ; to which the count, who never argued, replied by two unanswerable reasons—" The affair is settled and you desired it." Then she changed her tactics, and tried the effect of threats. She swore she would break with him, leave him, recal her child, make a scandal, die. The little lady was charming in her wrath ; she had the air of an angry canary, to which a lover could not remain insensible. The count asked for mercy, but without giving up his resolution in the slightest degree. He bent like those good steel springs which are moved by a great effort, but fly back to their place with the speed of lightning. Then she opened the dam of her tears ; she exhausted the arsenal of her tenderness. For three-quarters of an hour she was the most unhappy and loving of women. You would have believed on hearing her that she was the victim and Germaine the executioner. Don Diego wept with her ; tears ran down his masculine face, like rain down a bronze statue. He gave way to all those acts of cowardice which love imposes. He spoke of the future countess with a coldness bordering on contempt : he swore on his honour that she would not live long. He offered to show her to Madame Chermidy before his marriage. But his word was given and the Villaneras never withdraw from what they have once said. All the lady could obtain was that he would come and see her every day up to the mar-

riage, clandestinely, without the knowledge of any one
—above all, his mother.

The next day the countess took him to Sanglié
house, and presented him to his new family. It was
a visit of ceremony, that lasted a quarter of an hour
at the most. Germaine nearly fainted when presented
to him. She said afterwards that his harsh face
frightened her, and she fancied she saw in him her
sexton. As for him, he was ill at ease ; still he found
some words of politeness and gratitude by which the
duchess was affected.

He called every day while the banns were being
put up, without his mother, and brought a bouquet,
according to the established custom. Germaine begged
him to choose scentless flowers, for she could hardly
bear the fragrance. These daily interviews troubled
him much, and wearied Germaine ; but custom had
to be obeyed. The doctor feared for a moment that
his patient would succumb before the appointed day,
and his fears affected Madame Chermidy. When she
saw that Germaine was really given over, she was
afraid lest she might die too soon, and took an interest
in her life. At times she conveyed the count to the
house, and waited for him in her carriage.

The duchess said that her daughter could not be
married from rooms over a stable, so she hired some
handsomely furnished rooms near at hand. Germaine
was carried to them without misadventure on a sun-
shiny day. There Don Diego came to pay his court to
her, and the dowager called oftener than he did, and
remained longer. She soon learned to read the duchess's

heart, and the ice was broken. She admired the virtues of this noble woman who, for eight years, had endured so much without a stain. For her part the duchess recognised in the dowager one of those chosen souls which the world does not appreciate, because it stops at the covering. Germaine's bed served as the point of union for these two mothers. The old countess frequently disputed with the duchess the painful and disagreeable duties of sick nurse. They vied with each other in undertaking those fatigues in which the devotion of the sublime sex is so brilliantly displayed.

The old duke caused his wife additional cares which she would gladly have been spared. Money had restored him a third youth—an inexcusable youth—whose cold and degrading follies interest nobody. He was always out, and the duchess, in her discreet solicitude, did not dare to inquire about his actions. He said he was trying to find some relief from his domestic annoyances. His daughter's gold slipped through his fingers, and who can say what hands picked it up! He had lost during eight years of wretchedness, that necessity for elegance which salves over the follies of a well-born man. All pleasures were alike to him, and he even brought the fulsome odours of a pot-house to Germaine's bedside. The duchess trembled at the idea of leaving this old vagrant in Paris with money enough to kill a dozen men. There could be no thought of taking him to Italy, for Paris was the only place in which he had known life, and his heart was attached to the asphalt of the Boulevards. The poor

woman felt herself distracted by two contending
duties. She would gladly have torn herself in two, to
soothe the last moments of her daughter, and bring
back the erring old age of her incorrigible husband.
Germaine saw from her bed the internal struggles
torturing her mother. Through suffering together
they had learned to understand each other without
speaking, and had only one mind between them. One
day the sick girl declared positively that she would
not leave France. "Am I not well enough here," she
said; "what need flaring on the high road a candle
which is rapidly expiring?"

The dowager entered upon this with the count and
M. Le Bris.

"Dear countess," Germaine said, "so you insist on
taking me to Italy? I am much better here for what
I have to do, and I should not like my mother to
leave Paris."

"Well, let her remain," the dowager said, with her
Spanish vivacity; "we do not want her, and I will
take care of you better than any one can. You are my
daughter, hark you, and we will prove it."

The count insisted on the journey, and the doctor
coincided with him. "Besides," the latter added, "the
duchess will not be particularly useful to us. Two
patients in one carriage do not advance matters.
The journey is good for you, but would fatigue the
duchess."

In the bottom of his heart the good fellow wished
to spare the duchess the sight of her daughter's dying
moments. It was settled, therefore, that the duchess

should remain in Paris, while Germaine went off with her husband, mother-in-law, and doctor.

M. le Bris had agreed somewhat hastily to give up his practice. The journey might cost him dearly if it lasted any length of time. The difficulty was not to find a doctor who would take charge of the duchess and his other patients ; but Paris is a city where the absent are always in the wrong, and a man who does not put himself in evidence every day is soon forgotten. The young doctor had a hearty friendship for Germaine, but friendships never carry us so far as self-forgetfulness. That is one of the privileges of love.

For his part, Don Diego was anxious to do his duty nobly, and he wished Germaine to be accompanied by her regular physician. He asked M. le Bris how much he earned a year.

" Eight hundred pounds," said the doctor ; " out of that I receive two hundred or two hundred and fifty pounds."

" And the rest ?"

" Is outstanding. We doctors do not have recourse to the County Court."

" Will you undertake this journey to Italy for eight hundred pounds a year ?"

" My poor count, do not talk of years. The remainder of her days may be counted by months, perhaps by weeks."

" Well, then, say eighty pounds a month, and come with us."

M. le Bris agreed. Self interest is, after all, mingled in all human affections. It plays its part in the farce

as well as in the tragedy. In our streets crime and
virtue, deep and dark, never come in collision without
elbowing a brilliant and sonorous personage called
" money."

The doctor was requested to hand the duke the price
of his daughter. Don Diego would never have managed
to give a gentleman money ; but M. le Bris, who knew
the duke, performed the commission easily. He gave
him an order on the funds for two thousand pounds
a-year, saying simply,—

" My lord, this represents the Duchess's health."

" And mine," the old gentleman added.   " You
have rendered us a service, doctor, and I wish to attach
you to my house."

The young man replied, with much fervour—

"That is already done, my lord."

He had attended them all for three years without
receiving a shilling.

On the morning of the wedding-day Germaine's dress
was tried on. She lent herself gently to this sorry
jest. The milliner saw that the point of the body had
come unsewed.

" I will repair it," she said.

" What matter !" the sick girl remarked.   " I shall
not wear it out."

Her veil and head-dress were brought, and she
noticed the absence of the orange blossoms. " That is
right," she said ; " I was afraid something might be
forgotten."

The Duchess melted into tears. Germaine begged
her pardon for her cowardice.

" Wait," she said ; " you shall see me in presence
of the enemy. I will bear your name with honour, for
am I not the last of the La Tours ?"

Don Diego's witnesses were the Spanish ambassador
and the chargé d'affaires of the Two Sicilies ; Germaine's, the Baron de Sanglié and Doctor le Bris. The
whole Faubourg was invited to the marriage ceremony.
M. de Villanera knew the best people in Paris, and the
old duke was not sorry to resuscitate publicity as a
millionaire. Three-fourths of the persons invited were
punctual, for in spite of the discretion of the parties
interested, the public suspected something. At any
rate, the marriage of a dying girl is always a rare and
curious sight. When midnight struck, two or three
hundred carriages, which had arrived from the ball or
the theatre, put down their loads on the little square of
St. Thomas Aquinas.

The bride was carried from the carriage by Dr. le
Bris. She appeared to be not so pale as had been
expected. She had begged her mother to put her on
some rouge to play this farce. She walked with a firm
step to the cushion arranged for her. Her father gave
her his hand, and marched triumphantly by her side
while looking at the spectators. The strange old
man could not refrain from an exclamation, on seeing in the crowd a charming face, half-veiled. He
said, as if he was in the park, " What a pretty
woman !"

It was Madame Chermidy who had come to judge
for herself how long the bride had still to live.

After the ceremony, a carriage with four horses

conveyed the travellers to the Fontainebleau gate, but it turned back there, and drove to the count's town house. It was necessary to fetch little Gomez, and give Germaine some hours' rest. Dr. le Bris put the bride to bed.

CHAPTER IV.

THE TOUR IN ITALY.

GRRMAINE slept but little on the first night of her marriage. She was lying in a large curtained bed, in the middle of a strange room. An old-fashioned lamp, suspended from the ceiling, threw a dim light on the paper that covered the walls. A thousand grimacing faces detached themselves from the wall, and seemed to dance around the bed. For the first time during twenty years she was separated from her mother. Her place was taken by the Dowager Countess—a great attentive shadow, but so ugly as to cause terror. In a scene so disheartening the poor child dosed, neither asleep nor awake. She closed her eyes, not to see the walls, but opened them again directly. Other figures more horrifying still, glided beneath her very eyelids. She fancied she saw Death in person, as he is drawn in the mediæval missals.

"If I go to sleep," she thought, "no one will come to wake me; I have been placed here to die."

A large buhl clock marked the hours on the chimney. The dull stroke of the pendulum, the ticking of the works, affected her nerves, so she begged the countess to stop the clock. But soon silence appeared to her more terrible than the sound, and she begged that life might be restored to the innocent machine.

Toward morning, fatigue grew more powerful than alarm. Germaine let her weary eyelids fall, but raised them again, and saw, with terror, that her hands were crossed on her chest. She knew that the dead are buried in this position. She threw her little thin arms out of the clothes and clutched at the frame of the bed, as if holding on to life. The countess took possession of her right hand, kissed it gently, and kept it on her knees. Then, at last, the sick girl fell asleep, and dreamed till daybreak. She fancied that the countess was standing at her right hand, with white wings and an angelic face. On her left was another woman, whose face it was impossible to imagine. All she could distinguish was two large Cashmere wings and diamond claws. The count was walking about in a state of great agitation ; he went from one woman to the other, and each whispered in his ear. At length the heavens opened ; a pretty chubby boy came down, resembling those little cherubs that guard the tabernacle in churches. He flew towards her with a smile—she held out her arms to receive him, and the movement she made aroused her.

When she opened her eyes, a curtain was noiselessly drawn, and she saw the old countess enter in travelling dress, with little Gomez trotting at her side. The child smiled instinctively on the pretty little pale lady, with her golden locks, and tried to climb up the bed. Germaine attempted to lift him, but was not strong enough. The countess picked him up like a feather, and laid him gently among his new mother's pillows.

"My daughter," she said, with badly-restrained emotion, "I present to you the Marquis de los Montes de Hierro."

Germaine took the boy's head in her hands, and kissed him twice or thrice. Little Gomez submitted to it ; I even fancy he returned a kiss. She looked at him for a long time, and felt her heart moved. I cannot say what was working at the bottom of her thoughts, but after an invisible effort, she said, in a low voice, "My son !"

The dowager kissed her for this kind word.

"Marquis," she said, "this is your little mother."

The child repeated, with a smile, "Mother."

"Would you like me," Germaine said, "to be your mother ?"

"Yes !"

"Poor little fellow, it will not be for long. No !"

"No !" the boy repeated, without knowing what he said.

From this moment mother and son were friends. Little Gomez would not leave her room, and was present by right at Germaine's toilet. She was holding him on her knees when the count came in to wish his wife good day and kiss her hand. She experienced a species of shame at being thus surprised, and let the child slip off on to the carpet.

Germaine had never loved but her father and mother She had not been to a boarding-school ; she had had no friends. She had not seen in the parlour the grown-up brothers of her schoolfellows. That squandering of love and friendship which takes place at boarding-schools, and which wears out the hearts of young girls prematurely, had not attacked the riches of her soul.

Hence she loved her mother-in-law and son like a prodigal who has no fear of ruin. She gave Dr. le Bris a sisterly friendship; but it seemed to her impossible to love her husband; that alone was beyond her strength, and she had better give up all thoughts of it. Not that the count was a disagreeable man; any other than Germaine would have found him perfect. Of all her companions he was assuredly the most patient, attentive, and delicate. A knight of honour charged with the escort of a young queen could not have performed his duties better. He arranged everything for the journey and the halt; he regulated the pace of the horses, chose the lodgings, and saw that the rooms were ready. They made two journeys a day of fifteen miles each, with a long halt between.

This mode of travelling would wear out the patience of a young and healthy man, but Don Diego was only afraid of going too fast and fatiguing Germaine. He was a smoker, as I think I told you: from the first day of the journey he only smoked two cigars a day—one in the morning before starting, the other at night before going to bed. But one morning the patient said to him—

"Have you not been smoking? I smell it in your clothes."

He left his cigars at the first inn they came to, and smoked no more.

The sickly girl accepted everything from her husband without thanks. Had she not given him more than ever he could repay? She constantly repeated to herself that Don Diego was attentive to her through duty— as a salve to his conscience; that friendship took no part in his attentions; that he was coldly playing the part of a good husband; that he loved another woman; that he had left his heart in France. Lastly, she thought that this man, so careful to keep her alive, had married her in the hope that she would soon die, and she was indignant at seeing him employ all his efforts to retard an event which was the object of all his wishes.

She was as harsh to him as she was gentle to all the rest. She sat in the back of the carriage with the dowager. Don Diego, the doctor, and the child, sat with their backs to the horses. If the child clambered on her knees, or the dowager, lulled to sleep by the monotonous motion, let her head fall on her thin shoulder, she would play with the child or nurse the countess; but she would not even permit her husband to ask her how she was.

One day she answered him with cutting cruelty, "All is going on well; I am suffering greatly." Don Diego looked out at the scenery, and his tears fell on the wheel.

The journey lasted three months without altering either Germaine's health or temper. She grew no better or worse, she dragged along. She was still severe to her husband, but was growing accustomed to him. All Italy passed by the side of the carriage—yet she took no interest in anything, and would not settle down. It is true that in winter Italy is very like France; it may freeze a little less, but it rains a good deal more.

The climate of Nice would have done her much good, and Don Diego had hired a pretty rose-painted villa, on the English quay, with a garden of orange trees covered with fruit. But she grew vexed at seeing a whole population of consumptive people pass the live-long day. Hopeless patients exiled to Nice frighten one another, and each read her fate in the pallor of her neighbour.

"Let us go to Florence," she said.

Don Diego had the horses put to at once.

She found that this city had a festal air, which seemed to mock her misfortune. The first time she was taken to the Promenade, where she heard the bands of the Austrian regiments, and chubby flower girls threw bouquets at the carriage, she harshly reproached her husband for having exposed her to so cruel a contrast. Pisa was the next place she was carried to. She wished to see the Campo Santo and Orcagna's fearful masterpiece. These funereal paintings, these pictures of death as master of life, struck her imagination—she left the place more dead than alive.

She expressed a desire to go as far as Rome. The climate of that great city could not benefit her much, but she seemed to have reached that stage when a physician no longer refuses anything to his patient.

She saw it once, and fancied she was entering a vast Necropolis. These deserted streets, empty palaces, and mighty churches, in which one communicant may be seen kneeling, assumed, in her eyes, a sepulchral physiognomy.

She went to Naples, and was no better there. The most lovely bay in the world rolled and unrolled its blue waters before her; Vesuvius smoked beneath her windows—the place was well chosen either to live or die. But she could not endure the horses in the street —the shrill cry of the coachmen—the clanking tread of the Swiss patrols—and the songs of the fishermen. She detested this noisy, bustling city, where a person is not permitted even to suffer in peace. Don Diego offered to look for a more quiet spot in the neighbourhood, but she insisted on seeking it herself, and so expended her strength that she was worn out in a few days. The doctor was annoyed that she had endured such fatigue; nature must have constructed her body of solid materials, or a very vigorous mind retarded the ruin of the tottering edifice.

She was shown Castellamare and Sorrento, and taken from village to village for a week, without making any choice. One evening she had a fancy to visit Pompeii by moonlight.

"It is just the town to suit me," she said, with a bitter smile; "it is but just that ruins should console each other!"

They were obliged to drag her about for two hours over the uneven pavement of the dead city. It is a delicious walk for a healthy mind. The day had been lovely—the night was quite limpid. The moon illuminated objects like a winter sun. Silence added to the sight a gentle and solemn charm. The ruins of Pompeii have not the crushing grandeur of those Roman monuments which inspired Madame de Staël with such long sentences. It is the residue of a town of two thousand souls. The public and private edifices possess a provincial physiognomy. On entering these narrow streets, and visiting these cottages, you penetrate into the inner life of antiquity; you are received as a friend among a people no longer in existence.

You find there a singular mixture of that artistic feeling which distinguished the ancients, and that bad taste which is peculiar to little shopkeepers of all times. Nothing is more pleasant than to discover, beneath the dust of twenty centuries, gardens like those at the Invalides, with the microscopic fountain, the marble ducks, and the statuette of Apollo in the centre. Such was the abode of a Roman citizen, living on his savings in the year 79 of the Christian era. The doctor's merry humour had full scope among these curious relics. Don Diego translated to his wife the interminable stories of the keeper. But the sick girl's febrile impatience destroyed all the pleasure of the trip. The poor girl was no longer mistress of herself; she was the prey of her illness and approaching death. She only walked to feel she was alive, and only spoke to hear the sound of her own voice. She went on, turned back, wanted to see what she had already seen, stopped on the road, and invented caprices which no one could satisfy.

About nine o'clock she felt cold, and proposed returning to the inn. " Decidedly," she said, " I wish to die
here ; I shall be quiet." But she remembered that
Vesuvius was not quite expended yet, and might pour
a bed of fire over her tomb. She spoke of returning
to Paris, and retired to bed with a shudder of evil
omen.

The dowager supped by her bedside ; the child was
asleep long ago. The landlord of the *Iron Crown*
invited the two gentlemen to come down into the coffee
room ; they would be more comfortable there than in
a sick room, and would have company. The doctor
accepted, and Don Diego followed him.

The company was reduced to two persons ; a stout
French painter, a jolly fellow, and a young Englishman,
as rosy as a prawn. They had seen Germaine enter,
and guessed without difficulty of what malady she was
dying. The painter possessed a gay philosophy, like
a man whose digestion is good. " I, sir," he said to
his neighbour, " if ever I am affected in the chest, which
is not very likely, will not budge a foot from Paris.
People recover everywhere, and die everywhere. The
air of Paris, perhaps, suits pulmonary complaints better
than any other. People talk of the Nile ; the landlords
at Cairo spread that report. Of course the steam of the
river is good for something, but you forget the desert
sand. It enters into your lungs, lodges there, collects,
and good-bye ! You will reply, if a man must die he
has the right to choose the spot. That is an idea I
quite understand. Have you ever travelled in the
Regency of Tunis ?"

" Yes!"

" Did you happen to sec a man's head cut off there?"

" No!"

" Well, then, you lost something. Those are people who insist on choosing their place for dying. When a Tunisian is condemned to death, he is given till sunset to choose the spot where he would like to have his head cut off. Early in the morning two executioners take him by the arms, and lead him into the country, each time they arrive at any pretty spot, a fountain or two palm trees, the executioners say to the patient, ' How do you like that? You cannot find a nicer place.' ' Let us go a little further,' says the other, ' there are flies here.' Thus they walk about till he has found a place to suit him, and he generally makes up his mind at sunset. He kneels, his neighbours draw their knives, and cut off his head in the most familiar manner. But he has the consolation of dying on a spot of his own choice.

" I knew at Paris a ballet girl, in very good health, who had the same mania. She was offered a site at Père la Chaise. She went to see it now and then, and always with increased pleasure. Her six yards were situated in one of the pleasantest parts of the cemetery, surrounded by highly respectable tombs, and with a fine view of the high road. But you English are the queerest fish in that respect. I met one who wished to be buried at Etrétat, because the air is so pure, there is such a fine view of the sea, and it was never visited by cholera. I heard of another who bought a burial site in every country he passed through, so that he might not be taken unawares. Unfortunately he died while crossing from Liverpool to New York, and the captain threw him into the sea."

Don Diego and the doctor could have wished anything else than this to be talked about, and were about to beg their neighbours to change the topic, when the young Englishman said,

"I, sir, was ill just two years ago like the young lady who passed us. The doctors of London and Paris signed my passport, and I went in search of a grave. I chose the Ionian Islands, in the southern part of Corfu. I installed myself there while awaiting my hour, and I felt so comfortable that the hour passed by."

The doctor interrupted him with that carelessness prevalent at public tables in Italy, "You were consumptive, sir?"

"In the third stage, unless the faculty humbugged me."

He quoted the names of the doctors who gave him over. He told how he had ended by attending to himself, without any fresh remedies, while awaiting death beneath the sky of Corfu.

M. le Bris asked permission to employ the stethoscope, but he refused with comic terror. He had heard the story of the physician who killed his patient in order to find out how he recovered.

An hour later the count was sitting by Germaine's bed. Her face was red, and she was catching her breath.

"Come here," she said to her husband, "I wish to speak with you seriously. Do you notice that I am better to-night? I am, perhaps, on the road to recover. Your future prospects would be ruined. Suppose I were to live! I have already made you pine three months; no one expected it. We cling to life in our family; you will have to kill me. You have the right to do it, I know—you paid for it. But grant me a few days longer, the light is so lovely; I fancy that the air is becoming softer to breathe."

Don Diego took her hand; it was burning.

"Germaine," he said, "I have just dined with a young Englishman, whom I will present to you to-morrow. He was worse than you, he assured me, but the sky of Corfu cured him. Would you like to go to Corfu?"

She sat up in bed, looked at him fixedly, and said with an emotion that had something delirious in its nature,

"Do you speak the truth? I can live? I shall see my mother again? Ah, if you save me my whole life will be too short to pay so much gratitude. I will serve you as a slave, I will educate your son, I will make him a great man. Wretched woman that I am! It was not for that you chose me; you love that woman, you regret her, you write to her, you are longing for the moment to see her again, and every hour I live is a robbery from you."

She was frightfully ill for two days in this inn room, and it was believed that she would die in the ruins of

Pompeii. Still she was enabled to rise in the first week of April. She was taken to Naples, the party embarked in a steamer proceeding to Malta, and thence an Austrian Lloyd's conveyed them to the port of Corfu.

CHAPTER V.

THE DUKE.

THE duke and duchess bade farewell to their daughter in the vestry room. The duchess wept copiously. The duke took the separation more gaily, to reassure his wife and daughter ; it might be, though, because he did not have any tears ready to hand. In his heart he did not expect Germaine would die ; only he and the old countess believed in the miracle of her cure. This Cicisbeo of fortune was firmly convinced that one piece of good luck never comes singly. All seemed to him possible since he had once more gained the upper hand, and the vein had returned to him. He began by predicting the recovery of his wife, and the result proved him right.

The duchess possessed a strong constitution, like the whole of her family. Fatigue, watching, and privation, had played a great part in the critical illness age had brought upon her. To these must be added the daily anguish of a mother who is awaiting her daughter's last sigh. The duchess suffered as much, and more, from Germaine's condition than from her own. When separated from her beloved patient she gradually recovered, and was less painfully affected by sufferings she no longer witnessed. Imagination causes us to suffer just as much as feeling does; but a misfortune out of our sight loses some of its crushing effect. If we see a man run over in the street, we experience a physical shock just as if the vehicle had wounded ourselves, but reading of the accident in the *Times* produces but a slight sensation. The duchess could be neither happy nor calm; but, at least, she escaped the direct action of danger in her nervous system. She was never completely re-assured, but she no longer lived in the expectation of her daughter's last sigh. She never opened a letter from Italy without trembling; but, between the arrival of the letters, she had moments of respite. The sharp agony that had tortured her was now followed by a dull grief, with which habit rendered her familiar. She experienced that sorrowful relief of the patient who has passed from an acute to a chronic stage.

A friend of the young doctor visited her twice or thrice a week; but her real physician was still M. le Bris. He wrote to her regularly, as well as to Madame Chermidy, and though he strove never to set down a falsehood, the two correspondences bore no resemblance to each other. He repeated to the poor mother that Germaine lived, that the malady was arrested, and that this happy suspension of a fatal progress might render a miracle possible. He did not boast of curing her, and said to Madame Chermidy that Heaven alone could indefinitely adjourn Don Diego's widowhood. Science was impotent to save the young Countess of Villanera. She was still living, and the disease seemed to have stopped on the road, but, like a traveller who rests at an inn, to progress more quickly the next day. Germaine was still weak during the day, feverish and excited on the approach of night ; sleep refused her its consolations ; appetite came to her in fits and starts, and she rejected dishes with disgust as soon as she had tasted them. Her thinness was terrifying, and Madame Chermidy would not be sorry to see her. Her limpid and transparent skin revealed each bony prominence and each muscular development, and her cheek-bones seemed to start out of her face. Indeed, Madame Chermidy must be very impatient if she asked for anything better.

The duke was already celebrating the recovery of his daughter by various rejoicings. At the age of wisdom, this old man, whose white hairs would have been respected if he had not dyed them, resisted better than a young man all the fatigues of pleasures. It could be easily seen that he would sooner come to the end of his money than of his wants and strength. Men who have entered on life at a late age find extraordinary reserves for their last years.

He had but little ready money, though he possessed so large a fortune. The first half of his annuity would not be due till July 22nd ; in the meanwhile, he must live on Germaine's one thousand pounds. It was sufficient for the housekeeping and those little debts which wait less patiently than the great ones. If the duchess had had the disposal of this little fortune, she would have placed the house on an honourable footing, but the duke had always kept money under lock and key at the time when there was any in the house. He paid but few of the creditors, he politely refused to buy furniture, and, in defiance of the duchess and common sense, kept on a suite of rooms at five hundred pounds a year, in which he was hardly ever visible. Now and then he gave Semiramis a sovereign for kitchen expenses, but never dreamed of asking what wages were owing her. He bought the duchess three or four magnificent dresses, when she wanted the most indispensable articles of under-clothing. What he spent daily for his personal expenses was a secret between himself and his strong box.

You must not believe, however, that he displayed that odious egotism of certain husbands, who spend money without counting it, and wish to know to a halfpenny their wives' outlay. He granted the duchess as much liberty for minor expenses as he reserved to himself for great ones. He was ever the polished, tender, and attentive husband whom the poor lady adored even in his faults. He inquired after her health with almost filial attention. He repeated to her, at least once a day, that she was his guardian angel. He gave her such gentle names that, had it not been for the testimony of the mirrors, she might have fancied herself still twenty. That is something, after all ; the worst husband is only half contemptible when he leaves his victim on sweet illusions. A great artist who saw our society with the eyes of Balzac, and drew it better—Gavarni—has placed this singular verdict in the mouth of a low woman—"My husband, a perfect dog, — but the king of men !" Translate the remark into elegant language, and you

will understand the obstinate love of the duchess for
her husband.

Still, the old man rapidly went down hill. When
the report of his new fortune spread through Paris,
he was hailed by a number of old acquaintances who
had been accustomed to turn their heads on meeting
him. He was invited to some of their saloons, where
the most honourable and elegant men sometimes carry
good company to seek bad. He saw here and there
furniture he had bought; he inquired the hour from
clocks for which he had paid the bill. The rage for
play, which had slumbered in him for some years, now
re-awoke more ardent than ever; but he was a dupe
in those lurking places which the police now and then
sweep out. That dangerous world which excels in
following all the vices by which it lives, prepared a
triumphal reception for the returning duke. His
posthumous youth was admired, as it issued from
misery like Lazarus from the tomb. It was proved
to him that he was twenty years of age, and he tried
to prove it to himself. He began eating suppers
again to the great injury of his stomach, he drank
champagne, smoked cigars, and cracked his bottle.
New arrivals from the provinces, strangers wandering
about Paris, and young men just escaped from the
hands of their guardians, admired the high tone and
aristocratic bearing of the fallen gentleman. Many
respected him more than he respected himself—women
saw in him a ruin they had made, and which remained firm, spite of all. In some strata of society,
more importance is given to a man who has knocked

down a quarter of a million than to a soldier who has
lost both his arms on the field of battle.

The respect due to his name, which had accompanied him during the first half of his career, finally
abandoned him without chance of return. In two
months he became the most notorious scamp in Paris.
Perhaps he would have put more restraint on his conduct if any report of his behaviour could have reached
his family; but Germaine was in Italy, and the
duchess was shut up at home, so he had nothing to
fear.

The contrast between his name and his conduct
obtained him a degree of low-class popularity by which
he was intoxicated. He might be seen, on quitting
the theatre, in a café on the boulevard, surrounded by
blue-chinned actors and low comedians, who drank
punch in his honour, gazed on him with bleared eyes,
and disputed the honour of squeezing the hand of a
duke who had no pride about him. He fell lower still
if possible. He openly sat in pot-houses outside the
city, drinking the horrible red wine sold there. It is
very difficult in the nineteenth century to be an elegant
blackguard. Two or three foreign and French noble-
men have tried to revive these good old times, but it
proved a failure. The only debauches which can be
endured for any length of time are those which are
very expensive. Satisfaction with a wife, which is a
virtue among workmen, is the lowest degree of degra-
dation among men of pleasure.

The poor duke had reached the lowest stage, when
two persons held him out a hand, from very different

motives. These were the Baron de Sanglié and Madame Chermidy.

The baron called every now and then on the La Tours. He was their former landlord—Germaine's witness and friend of the family. He always found the duchess at home, but never the duke; but all Paris brought him news of his deplorable friend. He resolved to save him, as he had formerly lodged him, for the honour of the caste.

The baron is what may be termed a thorough gentleman; he is not handsome, and has something of the boar about his countenance. His large ruddy face is concealed behind a forest of red beard. He is as robust as a hunter, with a slight tendency to obesity, and would not be taken for more than forty, though he is really fifty. The Barons de Sanglié date from a period when men were solidly built. Rich enough to live well without doing anything, he treats himself as a friend; takes care of his person and enjoys himself. His costume and manners are equally aristocratic. In the morning you meet him in wide comfortable clothes of a coquettish negligence. In the evening he is irreproachable, without having the appearance of being dressed. He is one of those rare men whose attire never attracts attention; it seems as if their clothes grew upon them, and were the natural foliage of their persons. His overcoats are made in London, his frockcoats in Paris. He takes care of his body—that other garment of a gentleman. He rides every day, and plays rackets; at night he goes to the opera, and plays whist at his club. He is a famous companion, and splendid drinker; he is a great connoisseur in cigars — great amateur in pictures — good rider enough to win a steeple chase, but too wise to risk his fortune in a training stable: indifferent to new books, careless about politics, ready to lend to those who can repay, generous at times to those who have nothing, very blunt with men, most gallant to women; in a word, he is amiable and kind, like all intelligent egotists. To do good without inconveniencing yourself is a species of egotism, after all.

It was no easy task to save the poor duke, and the baron would never have succeeded without a powerful auxiliary in vanity. This passion still kept afloat amid the sad shipwreck of all aristocratic virtues, and M. de Sanglié seized him by that, as you would catch a drowning man by the hair.

He went to look for him in the dens where he was lowering his name and his caste. He tapped him roughly on the shoulder, and said to him with that frankness which so cleverly conceals flattery,—

"What are you doing here, my dear duke? This is not your place; everybody is asking after you in the Faubourg, men and women. All the La Tours have held rank there since Charlemagne, and I do not allow you any right to make your ancestors bankrupt. We all want you. Eh, by Jove! if you bury yourself here in the flower of your age, who will give us lessons in elegance? Who will teach us how to live grandly; to spend a fortune properly; and the art of pleasing women, which is growing more and more forgotten every day?"

The duke replied with a growl, like a drunkard awakened too soon. He was digesting his new fortune in peace. He had no desire to reassume those wearisome customs which the world imposes on its slaves. An invincible sloth enchained him to those facile pleasures which demand no dress, decency, or intelligence. He declared he was all right, wished nothing better, and that every man takes his pleasure where he finds it.

"Come with me," the baron went on, "and I promise to find you amusements more worthy of you. Do not be afraid of losing by the exchange. We live well, too, in our world, and no one knows it better than you do. You do not suppose I have come here to lead you home; in that case I should have sent you a parson. Hang it! I belong to your school too. I do not despise wine, play, or love; but I will maintain it against all comers, and against yourself, that a duke ought not to get drunk, ruin, or damn himself, save among his peers."

The old gentleman allowed himself to be converted by arguments of this nature. He went back—not to virtue, the road was too long for his old legs—but to elegant vice. The baron first took him to a great tailor, and he was fain to put on the livery of fashion. This singular patient still idolized his old person, but for some time he had cut down the expenses of the worship. He retained the custom of painting his face, and neglected none of the practices which could give him an appearance of youth, but he was not disinclined to appear fresher than his coat. It was proved to him, by a few yards of fine cloth, that a new coat regenerates, and he confessed to himself that tailors are not people to be despised. This was a great step in advance, for a man well dressed is half saved. Fathers of families are well aware of this fact, and when they come to Paris to tear a prodigal son from bad company, their first care is to take him to a tailor's.

The baron took on himself to launch his new pupil; he gained him admittance to his club, where there were good dinners, and the duke lost nothing by the change of cookery. Before his conversion the seasoned food of the pot-house and the use of adulterated drinks irritated his stomach, burnt his tongue, and condemned him to an inextinguishable thirst. He cheated it by drinking more, and the poor man had reached a state from which death alone could rescue him. The duchess was sometimes terrified by his burning breath, and though she dare not confess her fears, she discreetly placed by his bedside some fresh and perfumed drink which he was induced to swallow. The table d'hôte gradually restored him, although he gave up nothing; and his thirst for play kept him beneath the rod of his saviour. The members of the club played whist and écarté, boldly, but not rashly. The highest points at whist were a pound, and it was an arrangement without danger to a rich man. If he risked a heavy bet at an écarté table, no one had the right to recall him to reason, but, at least, they agreed to spare his purse. It was well known, and people took an interest in him, as in a convalescent. A gambler behaves like a wise man or a fool, according as he is thrust on or

restrained by those who surround him. The duke was
held back, and by so delicate a hand that he did not
feel the curb.

The most honourable salons opened their doors
widely to him. Every aristocracy has its freemasonry ;
and a duke, whatever he may have done, has impre-
scriptible claims to the indulgence of his equals. The
Faubourg St. Germaine, like the respectful sons of
Noah, threw a purple mantle over the man's back-
slidings ; men treated him with consideration ; women
with kindness. In what country have they ever
wanted in indulgence for scamps ? he was regarded
like a traveller who had passed through unknown
countries, still no woman ventured to ask him about
what he had seen. He reassumed without any embarrassment the tone of good society, for he combined,
with all the defects of youth, that flexibility of mind
which is its greatest ornament. He was found to be
a man worthy of his name and fortune, and M. de Villanera's choice of him as a father-in-law was generally
ratified.

The baron had promised him more lively pleasures,
and he kept his word. He did not shut him up in the
Faubourg as in a fortress, but introduced him to a less
stiff-necked generation. He led him to the verge of
the great world, into some of those salons which are
run down without proof, but not without reason. He
presented him to widows, whose husbands had never
come to Paris, or were said to be abroad in Government
service ; to women legitimately married, but who had
quarrelled with their family ; to marchionesses exiled

from the Faubourg on account of some scandal, and
to honourable persons who lived fashionably without
any known fortune. This class of society is bounded
by the world on one side, by the demimonde on the
other. I would not advise a mother to take her
daughter there, but many sons accompany their fathers
to these houses, and come away as they entered. You
do not find there the perfect tone and patriarchal life
of the old salons, but the dancing is perfectly proper ;
play goes on without cheating, and your great coat is
not stolen in the lobby. It was at one of these houses
that the duke was exposed to the blandishments of
Madame Chermidy.

She recognised him at the first glance, through
seeing him on the night of the marriage. She knew
that he was the grandfather of her · son, father of
Germaine, and a man of fortune at Don Diego's
expense. A woman of Madame Chermidy's stamp
never forgets the face of a man to whom she has given
a fortune. She had no objection to know him more
intimately ; but she was too clever to risk a step in
advance. The Duke saved her three fourths of the
journey. As soon as he learned who she was, he
introduced himself with an impertinence, the sight of
which would have gladdened the hearts of all the
respectable women in Paris. Nothing flatters virtuous
women more profoundly than to see those who are not
so treated cavalierly.

The Duke had no intention to insult a pretty woman,
and renounce in one day the religion of his whole
life ; but he spoke to people in their own language,

and thought he knew the nationality of Madame Chermidy. Hence, he seated himself familiarly by her side, and said—

"Madam, permit me to introduce to you one of your old admirers, the Duke de la Tour. I had the pleasure of seeing you once before at St. Thomas's Church. We are in some degree members of the same family—related through the children. Allow me as a blood relation to offer you the left hand of friendship."

Madame Chermidy, who reasoned with the rapidity of light, understood at the first word the position offered her. Whatever reply she might make, the Duke would remain the master of the field. Instead of accepting the hand he offered her, she rose with a movement of pain and dignity, which displayed all the graces of her form, and walked towards the door without turning her head, like a queen outraged by the meanest of her subjects.

The old gentleman was caught in the snare; he ran after her, and stammered some words in apology. She turned upon him a glance so brilliant, that he fancied he saw a tear in her eye, and then said to him in a low voice, with an emotion well suppressed or well feigned, " My lord, you do not know, you cannot understand. Call on me to-morrow at two; I shall be alone, and we will talk about it."

With these words she retired, like a woman who wishes to hear nothing further; and five minutes later her carriage drove off.

The poor duke had been warned: he knew the lady by heart, the doctor had painted her in her natural colours. But he reproached himself for what he had done, and lived till the morrow in a state of amazement, not quite exempt from remorse. And yet the proverb runs : "A man warned is worth two."

He was exact at the rendezvous, and found himself in the presence of a woman who had been weeping.

"My lord," she said to him, "I have done all in my power to forget the cruel words you addressed to me last evening. I have not quite recovered, but it will soon pass off ; let us say no more about it."

The duke wished to repeat his apologies, for he was in a state of profound admiration. Madame Chermidy had spent the morning in dressing herself irresistibly. She certainly appeared more lovely than on the previous evening at the ball ; for a woman in her boudoir is like a picture in its frame. She profited by the trouble into which her charms had thrown the duke, to wrap him in the folds of an irresistible logic. At first she employed the timid respect suitable to a woman in her position ; she evinced an exaggerated admiration for the family into which she had introduced her son ; she claimed the honour of having selected Madlle. de la Tour from among twenty great houses, and having raised once more one of the most glorious names in Europe. The voluptuous inflections and melancholy languor by which this speech was accompanied, persuaded the old man much better than her words did, and he had now no doubt that he had insulted his benefactress.

"I can understand," she exclaimed, "that you hold me in no great esteem. I am sure you would pity me, for you have a generous heart, if you but knew tho history of my life."

She had that expressive pantomime of the inhabitants of the south which adds so much of reality to the greatest falsehoods. Her eyes, her hands, her little quivering foot, spoke simultaneously with her lips, and seemed to bear witness in favour of her veracity. When once heard, you were as fairly convinced as if a court of inquiry had been opened and witnesses examined.

She described her birth as the daughter of a rich merchant in Provence. Her parents intended her hand and fortune for a rich tradesman, but love, that inflexible master of human lives, threw her into the arms of a simple officer. Her family withdrew from her, until the moment when M. Chermidy's brutality drove her from the conjugal abode. Poor Chermidy! a wife has always a safe game against a husband who is in China.

Once a widow, or nearly so, she came to Paris and lived there modestly till her father's death. An inheritance larger than she expected allowed her to maintain a certain rank ; some fortunate speculations increased her fortune, and she became rich. She was, however, the victim of *ennui;* for solitude is hard to bear at thirty. She loved the Count de Villanera from the first moment she saw him at the opera.

The duke could not help saying to himself that Don Diego was a deuced lucky fellow.

She then proved by arguments through which candour gleamed, that the count never gave her anything but his love. Not that he was deficient in

generosity, but she was only a woman, unable to confound the affairs of the heart with those of self interest.
She had carried her disinterestedness to the height of
a sacrifice; she had surrendered her son to the dowager
countess, and now abandoned him to another mother.
She had returned her lover his liberty, and he married;
he was striving to restore the health of his young wife,
and never even wrote to her, the deserted one, to give
her any account of little Gomez.

She ended her speech by letting her arms fall by her
side, with an action full of elegance. "And now,"
she said, "you see me more solitary than ever, suffering from that vacuity of heart which has already
ruined me once. There is no consolation; and though
I could find abundance of distractions, I have no heart
for pleasure. I know a few men of the world; they
come here every Tuesday evening to keep up the
spirit of conversation around my desolate fire; but I
dare not invite the Duke de la Tour to these melancholy
meetings, for I should feel humiliated by his refusal."

It is true that Madame Chermidy's bell did not
sound so correctly as that of Doctor le Bris, but the
vibration was so dulcet that the Duke allowed himself
to be deceived like a child. He pitied the pretty
woman, and promised to call now and then and bring
her news of her son.

Madame Chermidy's salon was, in fact, the meeting
place of a certain number of distinguished men, whom
she managed to attract by her clever devices. Some
knew her position, others believed in her virtue, but
all were persuaded that her heart was free, and that

the last possessor, no matter whether called Villanera
or Chermidy, had left an open succession. She took
advantage of her position to make all her admirers increase her fortune. Artists, authors, men of business,
men of the world, all served her in proportion to their
means. They were so many servants whom she paid
in hope. A stockbroker gained her a profit of one
hundred and fifty pounds a month ; a painter cheapened
pictures for her ; an enriched speculator secured her
good investments in land. Gratuitous services, if ever
there were such ; but not one of these men grew tired
of being useful to her, because none despaired of becoming dear to her. To those impatient persons who
pressed her too closely, she alleged her position ; they
could see that she lived in a glass house. She gave the
greatest publicity to her slightest actions, in order to
soothe Don Diego's susceptibility ; perhaps, too, to offer
a barrier to those who wished to compromise her in the
sight of the world.

The duke profited by the invitation granted him,
and his presence in her rooms was not without its
value for Madame Chermidy's reputation. It checked
certain rumours floating about as to the count's marriage ; it proved to some credulous beings that there
had never been anything between the latter lady and
M. de Villanera. How could it be supposed that
Madame Chermidy would invite his father-in-law, or
that he would visit her ?

She worked this new acquaintance as cleverly as the
old ones. It was of importance to her to know exactly
the state of Germaine, and the number of days she still

had to live; and thanks to her manœuvres, one fine day the duke entrusted to her all Doctor le Bris's letters.

The perusal of these letters produced in her such a revulsion that she would have been taken ill had she not been superior to all illness. She found herself betrayed by the doctor, the count, and nature. She imagined a future awaiting her the most odious the mind of a woman can conceive. A rival of her own choice would carry off her lover and her son, not only without crime, intrigue, or calculation, but with the support of every law, both divine and human.

Still she regained her courage in the thought that the doctor had wished to deceive the duchess. She wished to see Germaine's letters, and she calculated on the duke to satisfy this sinister curiosity.

The duke was a prey to one of those devouring passions which finish up the body and mind of old men. All the vices that had dragged him in various directions for the last half century had abdicated in favour of love. When engineers succeed in collecting in one channel all the streams dispersed over a plain, they create a river navigable by ships.

The baron, the duchess, and all who took an interest in him were astonished at the change in his manners. He lived as soberly as any ambitious young man who wishes to succeed with women. He was rarely seen at the club, and no longer played. His toilet occupied his mornings; he had taken to riding again, and went out from four till six. He dined with his wife whenever he was not invited to Madame Chermidy's. He went into society every evening to meet *her*, and so

soon as she retired he went home to bed. The fear of
compromising the woman he loved restored him to
those habits of discretion which had veiled the first disorders of his life, and the duchess fancied him out of
danger at the moment when he was irrevocably lost.

Madame Chermidy, a great artist in seduction, affected to treat him with filial tenderness. She received
him at any hour, even when dressing; she permitted
him to kiss her hand and forehead; she listened to him
kindly, accepted his caresses as marks of generosity,
evinced timidity, and did not seem to suspect the
brutal feeling, the flame of which she fanned every day.
To keep him at a distance she need only employ one
weapon, humility. She was pitilessly respectful. She
allowed him to call her by every endearing name that
love can suggest to a man, but she never once forgot to
call him "Your Grace." The poor old madman would
have sacrificed his whole fortue if Madame Chermidy
would only once have failed in her respect to him.

In the first place he sacrificed what any honourable
old man considers the dearest thing of all, the sanctity
of the paternal name. He borrowed from the duchess
Germaine's letters, under the pretence of reading them
again, and the noble woman wept with joy while confiding so dear a treasure to her husband. He ran with
them at once to Madame Chermidy's, and was received
with open arms. These letters, which the sick girl had
scrawled with her little trembling hand; these letters,
in which she did not fail to put some kisses for her
mother in a badly drawn frame beneath the signature;
these letters, which the duchess had bedewed with her

tears, were spread out like a pack of cards on a drawing table between a lost old man and a perverse woman.

Madame Chermidy, disguising her hatred behind a mask of compassion, greedily sought some signs of death among these protestations of affection, and was far from being satisfied. The odour extracted from this correspondence was not that which attracts the crows to follow an army. It was like the perfume of a little sickly flower pining beneath the winter blast, but which will expand in the sun if the southern breeze dispel the clouds. The cruel woman found that the hand was still very firm—the mind not yet a blank, and that the heart beat with dangerous vigour. This was not all ; she began to feel a strange suspicion. The sick girl described with too great satisfaction the attentions of her husband ; she accused herself of ingratitude ; she reproached herself with making a bad return for all that was done for her. Madame Chermidy grew furious at the thought that husband and wife might end by growing attached ; that pity, gratitude, association, might unite these two young beings, and that she might, one day, see sitting between Don Diego and Germaine, a guest she had not invited to the wedding—Love.

This profanation of Germaine's letters took place some days after her arrival at Corfu. Had Madame Chermidy been able to see with her own eyes her innocent enemy, it is probable that she would have felt less of fear than of pity. The fatigues of the voyage had thrown the poor girl into a deplorable state. But Don Diego's mistress incessantly summoned up monstrous visions of misery, and dreamed every night that she was hopelessly supplanted. When the day arrived that her suspicions were converted into certainty, she felt that she would be capable of any crime. In the meanwhile, through a feeling of prudence and vengeance, a want of amusement, and a spirit of calculation and perversity, she set to work stripping the duke. She found a pleasure in taking back the fortune she had given him, meaning to return it on the death of his daughter. There was some consolation in this, at any rate.

The difficulty was not to get hold of the securities; for the duke laid himself at her feet every day with all he possessed. He was of the temperament and character to ruin himself without saying a word, and conquer without proclaiming his victory. A well-bred man never compromises a woman, even if she has stripped him of every shilling. But Madame Chermidy thought it more worthy of her to take the fortune without giving anything in exchange, and while retaining her superiority over the giver.

One day, when the old man was raving at her feet, and repeating for the hundredth time the offer of his fortune, she took him at his word, and said, "I accept, my lord!"

The duke lost his head like a beginner in ballooning, who has just cut the rope of the balloon. He believed himself transported to the seventh heaven, but the lady gently checked his transports, and said—

"And when you have given me your fortune, do you think you will have paid me?"

He protested the contrary, but his eyes said with some

show of reason that when virtue puts itself up for sale, forty thousand pounds is not a bad price to pay for it.

She replied to her adversary's thought, " My lord, the women among whom you do me the injustice of reckoning me, fetch a higher price the richer they are. I was left one hundred and fifty thousand ; I have gained another hundred thousand by speculating, and my fortune is so thoroughly in hand, that I could realize it without loss in a month. You see, then, there are few women in France who have a right to set a higher price on themselves. This will also prove to you that I have it in my power to surrender myself for nothing. If I learn to love you sufficiently, and that is possible, money will be as nothing between us. The man to whom I give my heart will have the rest in the bargain."

The duke fell from his empyrean, and had a rude tumble. He was as unhappy at keeping his fortune as he had been delighted to receive it. Madame Chermidy seemed to take pity on him. " My great baby," she said, "do not cry. I began by telling you I would accept your fortune. But take care of yourself; I shall make my conditions."

The duke smiled like a man who sees heaven opening to receive him.

"It was I who enriched you," she said. " I had known you for a long period : at least I knew your reputation. You ruined yourself with a greatness worthy of heroic ages. You are the representative of the real nobility in this degenerate age. You are also, without being conscious of it, the only man in Paris

capable of inspiring women with a serious interest.
I have always regretted that you had not an incalculable
fortune, like Don Diego, for you would have been
greater than Sardanapalus : I did all in my power : I
enabled you to obtain forty thousand pounds. But
events have not fulfilled my hopes. You have a piece
of paper in your money-box of no service to you. You
will receive one thousand pounds on June 22nd ; till
then you will be forced to vegetate. You will run in
debt, and your income will only enrich your creditors.
Give me your securities, and I will have them sold by
my broker. I will take charge of the capital, and you
may make your mind easy, you will never see it again.
On the other hand, you must absolutely accept the
interest, but it will not be two thousand pounds ; you
will, in all probability, receive four thousand pounds,
or more. I am thoroughly acquainted with all the
goings-on on the Exchange, although women are not
admitted there; but I know that with several thousands
in cash, a person can gain as much as he likes. Investments in the funds are an admirable invention for
middle-class people who wish to live modestly and
without care, but for people of our condition, who fear
neither danger nor work, long live speculation ! It is
gambling on a grand scale, and you are a gambler, I
believe ?"

" I was so."

" You are so still ! We will be partners; we will
share our interests, our pleasures, our hopes, our fears."

" We will be only one."

" On the Exchange, at least."

" Honorine !"

Honorine appeared plunged in profound thought, and hid her face in her hands. The duke seized her wrist and put an end to this eclipse of beauty. Madame Chermidy gazed on him fixedly, indulged in a melancholy smile, and said :—

" Pardon me, my lord, I forget these castles in the air. We were losing our way in the future like the Children in the Wood. It was a fair dream—well, let us think no more of it. I must not strip you, I came to enrich you. What would be said of me?—what would you think of me, yourself? Suppose the duchess was to learn our compact?"

Madame Chermidy was well aware that in order to render a wife odious to her husband, it is only necessary to pronounce her name at a certain moment. The duke replied haughtily that his wife understood nothing of business, and that he had never allowed her to interfere.

" But," the temptress continued, " you have a daughter. All that you possess must come to her ; I am doing her a wrong."

" Well !" the duke replied, " and my daughter has a son who is yours. Your fortune and mine will go together, to the little marquis. Are we not one family ?"

" You told me so once before, my lord. But on that day you caused me less pleasure than you do now !"

Madame Chermidy locked up the securities, and took care not to sell them. From that moment the duke was her partner, he had a right to ask money from her and would receive from her as much as he required, until further orders. It was all he could obtain from this generous and smiling visitor. Honorine took the most minute care of the old man. She made him leave the *suite* of rooms he occupied, she removed him and the duchess to the Champs Elysées, where she furnished a house for them ; she took care that nothing should be wanted, and even provided for the kitchen expenses. That done, she rubbed her little hands, and said with a laugh—

"I hold the enemy in a state of siege—and if ever war is declared, I will pitilessly starve them out!"

CHAPTER VI.

LETTERS FROM CORFU.

Dr. le Bris to Madame Chermidy.

"Corfu, April 20, 1853.

"My dear Madame—I did not foresee, on the day that I took leave of you, that our correspondence would be so long, nor did Don Diego foresee it either. If I could have done so, I do not think he would have formed the heroic resolution of depriving himself of your letters, and of living without writing to you. But all men are subject to errors—physicians above all. By the way, do not show this sentence to any of my colleagues.

"We made a very stupid passage from Malta to Corfu, on board a remarkably dirty boat, in which the chimney smoked horribly. The wind was against us, the rain frequently prevented us from going on deck, and the waves poured into our berths. The sea-sickness only spared the child and the patient; mercies are vouchsafed to those who have just entered life, and those quitting it. Our only society was an English family just returned from India—a Colonel in the Company's service, and his two daughters, yellow as Russia leather. Madeira is the only thing that improves by such long voyages. These young ladies did not honour us with a single word; but there is some slight excuse for them in the fact that they could not speak a syllable of French. At the slightest break in the sky they went on deck to sketch scenery like plum-puddings. After an everlasting passage of five days, the vessel brought us safely into port; and we did not even have a shipwreck as a variety. Truly, the path of life is paved with deception.

"Until we can find quarters in the country, we are staying at the capital of the island, at the Victoria Hotel. We expect to leave it at the end of the week, but I cannot promise that we shall all go out on our feet. My poor patient is at the lowest ebb, for the voyage wearied her more than if she had suffered from sea-sickness. The dowager does not leave her for an instant. Don Diego is admirable. I do all I can; that is to say, very little. It is useless to attempt a treatment which would add to the suffering without any profit to the cure. How happy you are, Madame, to possess a beauty in such rosy health !

"If this crisis does not prove the last, I shall try ammonia or iodine. You will be therefore kind enough to order me Dr. Chartroul's apparatus, and a quantity of iodized cigars. Ammonia has also its merits, but the only remedy on which we can seriously count is a miracle. Hence, then, live in peace, love us a little, and help us to do our duty to the end. Old Gil, whom the dowager brought here to wait on her, caught a fever in Italy, though it is not the season for fevers. It is one patient more and a servant less.

"Joy and health have a magnificent representative

in the house in the shape of little Gomez. You will be very happy on the day you see him again. We fancy we can watch his growth, and that he is becoming, heaven pardon me, more good-looking. He will be less of a Villanera than was at first supposed. In fact, nature would be ungrateful not to grant him a share of his mother's beauty. He has outgrown his shyness, he lets you kiss him, and kisses you in return, and, in fact, is so affable that, were he a little girl, I should have reason to fear such precocity.

"Don Diego is bargaining with a descendant of the doges for a house that would suit him tolerably well. The country is divided into a number of petty estates, adorned with houses in a tottering condition. I visited some of the gardens, and found them generally more habitable than the houses attached to them. If we hire the Dandolo Villa we shall not be very badly off, for we shall only require to put in some panes of glass. The view is splendid, looking south on the sea. The neighbours are nobles, and some speak French, we are told ; but who knows whether we shall have time to form their acquaintance ?

"I shall not regret the town, though the life there is pleasant enough. It is pretty, and reminds me in some part of Naples. The Esplanade, the Palace of the Lord High Commissioner, and the environs form an English town. The English have built, at the expense of the Greeks, gigantic fortifications, which render the place a little Gibraltar. I go every morning to a parade of a Highland regiment, whose bagpipes form my happiness. The Greek town is ancient, and curiously built: lofty houses, small arcades, and a pretty face at every window. The Jew quarter is hideous; but there are pearls in this dungheap worthy the pencil of Gavarni. The population is Greek, Italian, Jew, Maltese, and is trying very industriously to become English. We have a theatre, at which the *Joan of Arc* of Maestro Verdi is performed. I went there one evening, when my patient's pulse was under 120. At the end of the first act, all the audience rose respectfully, while the band played "God save the Queen." This is a custom established in all English possessions. Do not be surprised that the death of Joan of Arc is represented before an English audience, for the author of the libretto took care to tone history down. Joan of Arc defends France against some enemies or other—Turks, Abyssinians, or Normans. She wears a cuirass of silver paper, and waves a flag the size of a fan, until the moment when a herald appears on the stage, to announce to the King that the enemy is routed. The heroine is brought in on cushions; a scarf stained with red indicates that she is mortally wounded. She rises with difficulty, and sings an aria, all with the upper register; after which she expires to the applause of the audience. All the inhabitants of Corfu are persuaded that Joan died of a wound and a roulade.

"The count let me go to the theatre alone, and yet you know how fond he is of Verdi. Was it not at a representation of *Hernani* that his eyes met yours for the first time? But the poor fellow literally sacrifices himself to his duty. What a husband, Madame, he will prove to the woman who becomes his real wife !

" The papers have brought us news from China, which you must have read with as much interest as we did. It seems that the most pug-nosed nation in the world has ill-treated two French missionaries, and that the *Naiad* has gone up to punish the culprits. If the *Naiad* has not changed her commander, we shall impatiently await news of the expedition. Each for himself and God for us all. I wish all imaginable prosperity to my friends, without desiring the death of any one. The Chinese are said to be bad artillerymen, although they boast of having invented gunpowder. Still it only requires a clear-sighted cannon-ball to render many persons happy.

" Good-bye, madame. If I were to write as I love you, my letter would never leave off. But, after the pleasure of gossiping with you, I must obey my duty, which summons me to the next room. Pleasure and duty ! Two horses very difficult to harness together. But I do my best ; and if I cannot reconcile everything, it is because a man has not free elbow-room between the anvil and the hammer. Love me, if you can ; pity me, if you will ; do not be angry with me, whatever may happen ; and if I were to send you, by the next post, a letter sealed with black, do me the honour of firmly believing that I have no claim on your gratitude.

" I kiss the prettiest hand in Paris.
" CHARLES LE BRIS."

The Countess Dowager of Villanera to the Duchess
de la Tour.

"Villa Dandolo, May 2, 1853.

" Dear Duchess—I am worn out, but Germaine is better. We all shifted our quarters this morning, or rather I moved them all. I had the boxes to pack, the patient to wrap up in cotton, the child to look after, to find the carriage, and almost to harness the horse. The count is fit for nothing ; but it runs in the family. There is a Spanish proverb : " As helpless as a Villanera." The little doctor buzzed round me like the fly on the coach-wheel, and I was obliged to make him sit down in a corner ; for when I am busy I cannot bear the zeal of anyone else ; it vexes me to be helped. And that ass of a Gil thought proper to catch the fever, though it was not his day out ! I am going to send him to Paris to be cured, and I must ask you to find me another. I did everything, foresaw everything, arranged everything for the best. I managed to be at once in doors and out ; in the town and in the house. At last, at ten o'clock, the whip cracks. Fortunately the roads are magnificent in this island. We rolled along on velvet to our villa, and here we are. I unpacked my people, opened the trunks, made the beds, and prepared dinner with a native cook, who insists on putting pepper in everything, even in bread and milk. They have eaten, and walked about the garden ; they are now sleeping, and I am writing to you from Germaine's bed-side, like a soldier on a drum on the evening of a battle.

"The victory is ours, on the word of an old captain! Our child will recover, or I will know the reason why! Still, she made me pass a very disagreeable fortnight in that town of Corfu. She could not make up her mind to sleep, and I had to treat her like an infant. She ate solely to please me ; nothing tickled her appetite ; and when you do not eat, good-bye to strength ; and she had only a breath of life left, which seemed ready to fly away at any moment ; but I would not let it. Have courage : she has dined this evening ; she has drunk a thimbleful of Cyprus and is asleep.

"I have often heard it said that a mother grows attached to her children in proportion to the grief they cause her ; but I did not know it from my own experience. All the Villaneras, from father to son, are as hardy as trees. But since you intrusted to me the poor body of this lovely soul, since I have watched by our child to prevent death approaching, since I have learned to suffer, breathe, and choke with her, I feel I have a heart. I was only half a mother until 1 had experienced the counterstroke of another's suffering. I am worth more, I am better, I am promoted. It is through suffering we draw nearer to the Mother of God, that model of all mothers—*Ave Maria, mater dolorosa !*

"Fear nothing, my poor Duchess. She will live. God would not have given me this profound love for her if He had resolved to move her from this earth. Providence sports with ambition, avarice, and all human passions ; but it respects legitimate affections ; it thinks twice ere it separates those who

love each other piously in the bosom of a family.
Why would it have attached me so closely to our
Germaine if it intended to kill her in my arms?
Besides, the interests of our family are bound up in
the life of this child-bride; if we had the misfortune
to lose her, Don Diego would form a low marriage
some day. No, no! Saint James, to whom he has
built two churches, will never suffer a name like ours
to be connected with that of Madame Chermidy.

"I hope nothing from Dr. le Bris; your clever men
do not understand how to cure the sick. The true
physicians are the angels in heaven, and on earth here.
Consultations, prescriptions, and all that is purchase-
able will not augment the number of our days. So
now I will tell you what we have imagined to obtain
our child a respite. Every morning, my son, my
grandson, and myself pray that Heaven will take
from our lives to add to that of Germaine. The boy
joins his hands with us, I pronounce the prayer, and
Heaven must be very deaf if it do not hear us.

"Don Diego loves his wife. I told you it would
be so. He loves her with a pure love, freed from all
earthly impurities. He feels for her that religious
adoration with which a good Christian endows the
saintly statue in his chapel. This is the way with us
Spaniards. We love simply, seriously, without any
worldly hope, with no other reward than the pleasure
of falling on our knees before a venerated image.
Germaine is nothing else; she is the perfect image of
the saints in Paradise.

"When she is cured, ah! then we shall see! Let

us only wait till the poor little pallid virgin has regained the hues of youth. At present her body is only a temple of transparent crystal, in which a soul is enshrined ; but when a regenerated blood courses through her veins, when the air of heaven expands her chest, when the generous perfumes of the country appeal to her heart, and make her temples beat ; when bread and wine have restored her strength, when impatient vigour makes her run beneath the orange trees in the gardens ; oh, then she will enter into a new phase of beauty, and Don Diego has eyes. He will draw a distinction between his old amours and his present happiness. I shall not need to show him how a noble and chaste beauty, heightened by all the brilliancy of blood, and all the splendour of virtue, is superior to the impudent charms of a profligate woman. He is on the right road ; for four months we have been away from Paris, she has not written, or received a letter from him. He is beginning to forget, while absent from the unworthy woman who was ruining him. Absence, which strengthens honourable love, kills, in the shortest conceivable time, that coarse passion of miscalled love which was only the result of association.

"Perhaps, too, our Germaine will be gained over by the contagion of love. Up to the present she only loves one of the whole family. I do not speak of the little marquis, for you know she adopted him from the very first day ; but she displays towards my poor son an indifference bearing a strong affinity to hatred. She does not ill-treat him more than she used to do,

and endures his attentions with a species of resignation. She suffers his presence, is no longer surprised
to see him by her side, and grows accustomed to him.
But it does not require a very strong sight to read on
her face a sullen impatience, a subdued hatred, which
revolts at times : it may be the contempt a virtuous
girl feels for a man who has been guilty of vice. I
fear, my poor friend, that to forget and forgive is a
virtue peculiar to our age ; young people do not prac-
tise it at all. Still, I must allow that Germaine carefully conceals her dislike and resentment. Her politeness to Don Diego is irreproachable. She talks with
him for hours without complaining of fatigue. She
listens to him talking. She answers sometimes. She
accepts his devotion with a cold and resigned gentleness. A less delicate man would not perceive that he is
hated ; my son knows it, and pardons it. He said to
me yesterday :—' It is impossible to detest one's friends
with more kindness and goodness. She is the angel
of ingratitude.'

"How will it all end ? Well, believe me, I have
confidence in heaven : I have faith in my son, and
good hopes for Germaine. We will cure her even of
her ingratitude, especially if you will come to our
assistance. I hear that the duke walks along the
path of virtue like a prize scholar, and that fathers
point him out as an example to their sons. If you
can take on yourself to leave him for a couple of
months, you will be received here with open arms, or in
case that your charming convert would also like to take
the country air, there is a house to let in our vicinity.

" Come soon, then, my excellent friend,—dear sister of my tenderness and afflictions. I love you more sincerely, in proportion as our daughter grows dearer to me. The distance that separates us cannot cool so firm a friendship, and even if we never met again or wrote to each other, our prayers would cross each other daily as they ascended to heaven.

"ISABELLA DE VILLANERA.

"P.S.—Do not forget my servant, and mind he must be young. Our Methuselahs at the Town-house would not grow acclimatized here."

Germaine to her Mother.

"Villa Dandolo, May 7, 1853.

"My dear Mamma—Old Gil, who will deliver you this letter, will tell you how comfortable we all are here. He did not catch the fever at Corfu, but in the Campagna, so you need not feel alarmed.

"I have been very ill since my last letter, but my second mother will have told you how much better I am. The count has also written to you, I dare say, but I never inquire about his actions. I have been strong enough for some time past, indeed, to blacken four pages of paper ; but will you really believe that I have no time ! I spend my life in breathing ; it is a most agreeable occupation which employs me ten or twelve hours a day.

"During the crisis I went through I suffered terribly. I do not remember ever having felt so bad in Paris, and I am sure that many persons in my place

would have wished for death, but I cling to life with
incredible obstinacy.   How people change ! and whence
comes it that I do not regard things in the same light ?

"It is doubtless because it would have been too sad
to die far away from you, not to have your dear hands
to close my eyes.   However, I did not want for care :
if I had succumbed, as the doctor rather expected, you
would have had one consolation.   The most terrible
thing on hearing of the death of those we love afar
from us, is the thought that they were not nursed as
they required.   For my part I want nothing, and
everybody is kind to me—even the count.   You
will remember that, my dear mamma, if any misfortune should happen to me.

"Perhaps, too, the friendship and compassion of
those who surround me have contributed a little to
attach me to life.   The day I said farewell to you and
my father, I said good-bye to everything.   I did not
know I was taking with me a real family.   The doctor
is admirable ; he treats me as if he hoped to cure me.

"The Countess of Villanera (the real one) is your
other self.   The marquis is an excellent little fellow;
and old Gil was full of attention.   I did not wish to
sadden all these people by the sight of my death, and
that is why I struggled so hard against it.   All the
worse for those who reckoned on my death,—they
will still have to wait.

"You asked me to describe our house, so that you
might know where to find me in your thoughts, when
you took a fancy to pay me a visit.   The Count, who
draws very well for a nobleman, will send you a sketch

of the house and garden. I took on myself to ask this favour of him ; but I should not have done it had it not been for you. In the meanwhile satisfy yourself with knowing that we inhabit a most picturesque ruin. At a distance the house resembles an old church de-molished during the Revolution. I would not believe that persons could be lodged in it. The house is approached by a long winding drive forming five or six terraces practicable for carriages, but the balus-trade on either side of the drive is in an awful state of dilapidation.

"It must hold together by the force of habit, for the mortar has been absent for a long time. Stocks and creeping plants nestle in all the crevices, and the road is as pleasantly scented as a garden. The house stands in the midst of trees, about a quarter of an hour's walk from the nearest village. I do not yet know exactly of how many floors it is composed ; the rooms are not above each other, and it looks as if the second floor had slipped down to the ground in an earthquake. On one side you enter direct, on the other you go down a breakneck incline. In the midst of this confusion you must seek your daughter, my dear mamma. I look for myself sometimes, and do not always succeed in the search.

"We have at least twenty unused rooms, and a magnificent billiard-room where the swallows build their nests. I ordered their nests to be left in peace, for what am I here myself?—a poor little marten chased by the cold. My room is the best in the whole house ; it is as large as the Chamber of Deputies, and

painted in oil from top to bottom,—I prefer that to
paper ; it is cleaner, and besides much fresher.   The
count procured me from Corfu entirely new furniture
of English manufacture.   My bed, my chairs, and my
sofa seem lost in the immensity.   The good countess
sleeps in an adjoining room with the little marquis.
When I say she sleeps, it is not to make her angry.
I see her at my side at the hour when I go to sleep.
I find her again at the same spot on opening my eyes ;
but I dare not tell her she has spent the night out of
her bed.   The doctor is a little further off on the same
floor ; he has been lodged as comfortably as was possible.   Those who take care of others, are accustomed
to take care of themselves.   M. de Villanera perches
I know not where under the roof.   But is there really
a roof? Our Greek and Italian servants sleep in the
open air, for it is the custom of the country.

" Long windows look out to the east and south, and
there are four of them.   The air and light are allowed
to enter at nine in the morning.   I am dressed, and
the windows are opened one after the other, lest the
sea breeze might reach me too suddenly.   At ten, I go
down into my gardens ; I have two, one to the north,
bounded by a wall more complicated than the great
wall of China ; and one on the south, bathed by the
sea.   The north garden is planted with olive trees,
jujube trees, and Japan medlars ; the other is an enormous thicket of orange, fig, and lemon trees, aloes,
cochineals, and gigantic vines which climb over all the
trees' and escalade all the heights.   The count said
yesterday that the vine is the goat of the vegetable

kingdom. It is a glorious thing, my poor mamma, to go wherever you like. I never knew that happiness, but if I live——!

"I begin to ·get about the walks bravely. They were impracticable a week ago, for Count Dandolo's gardener is a lover of the romantic and of picturesque confusion. The trees were cut down with an axe, just as in a primeval forest. I asked mercy for the orange trees; for you must know that I am reconciled with the perfume of flowers. Still I cannot bear them in a room yet, but only in the open air. The perfume of cut flowers expanding through a room mounts to my head like a deadly odour, and that saddens me; but when the plants are flourishing in the sun beneath the sea breeze, I rejoice with them. I share in their happiness, and I hail them as companions. How lovely the earth is!—how happy is everything that lives; and how sad it would be to leave the delicious world which God created for the pleasure of man. And yet there are people who kill themselves. What madmen!

"I was told in Paris that I should not see the leaves put forth. I should never have consoled myself for dying so soon without having seen spring. These dear little April leaves have come out, and I am still here to watch them. I touch them—I feel them—I nibble them, and say to them, 'I am still among you. Perhaps it may be granted me to pass the summer beneath their shadow. If we are destined to fall together, ah! then remain a long time on these beautiful trees —attach yourself firmly to the branches, and live, that I may live!'

"Unfortunately there are persons who would put on mourning at my recovery, and who would be inconsolable at seeing me live. What is to be done?—they are in the right. I have contracted a debt, and must pay it if I wish to be an honest girl.

"My dear mamma, what do people say in Paris about the count? what do you think of him? Is it possible that a man so simple, so patient, and so gentle, can be a wicked man? I noticed his eyes the other day for the first time; they are fine eyes, and people might be easily deceived.

"Adieu, my kind mother; pray for me, and try to persuade papa to go to church with you. If he did so for his little Germaine, the conversion would be complete, and I might perhaps be saved! But who would have credit in heaven more than yourself, dear angel!

"I am, with infinite affection, your loving daughter,

"GERMAINE.

"P.S. The kisses for my father are to the right of signature; yours on the left."

CHAPTER VII.

THE NEW SERVANT.

THE duke did not show Madame Chermidy the Countess's letter, but he handed her Germaine's to read. "You see," he said, "that she is half saved!"

She forced a smile, and replied, "You are a happy man; everything succeeds with you."

"Excepting love."

"You must have patience."

"Men of my age do not have it."

"Why not?"

"Because we have no time to lose."

"Who is the old Gil who brought the letter—a courier?"

"No! a man servant, whose place must be filled up Madame de Villanera requests the Duchess to find her a good servant."

"That is not easy in Paris."

"I will speak to my friend Sanglié's steward."

"Shall I help you as well? Lump has always half a dozen servants in her sleeve; she is a regular office for domestics."

"If Lump has any friend to set up in life, I have no objection to take him. But remember, he must be used to waiting on sick people."

"Lump will have one of that sort; she has every description."

Lump was Madame Chermidy's waiting maid. She was never seen in the drawing-room, even by accident; but the most intimate friends of the house would have been flattered to make her acquaintance; she was a woman of monstrous weight, a townswoman and cousin in some degree of Madame Chermidy. Her name was Honorine Lavinaze, like her mistress, and people had taken advantage of her deformity to nickname her "Lump." This living phenomenon—this pile of quivering fat—this female pachyderm, had followed Madame Chermidy and her fortunes for fifteen years. She had been the accomplice of her progress—the confidant of her sins—the receiver of her thousands. Seated at a corner of the fire, like a familiar monster, she read on the cards her mistress's fortune; she promised her the royalty of Paris, like one of Shakspeare's witches. She restored her courage, removed her annoyances, plucked out her grey hairs, and served with canine devotion. She had gained nothing while in service, had no money in the funds or in the savings bank, and wanted nothing for herself. Older than Madame Chermidy by ten years, and almost infirm through her fatness, she was sure of dying before her mistress and in her house; for people do not discharge a servant who can betray their secrets. In other respects Lump had no ambition, cupidity, or personal vanity; she lived in her beautiful cousin: she was rich, valiant, and triumphant in the person of Madame Chermidy. These two females, closely linked by a friendship of fifteen years, formed but one individual. It was a head with a double face, like the mask of the ancient comedians. On one side it smiled on love, on the other it grinned on crime;—one showed itself because it was lovely, the other hid itself because it would have terrified people.

Madame Chermidy told the duke she would attend to his business, and the same day she consulted with Lump as to the servant they could send to Corfu.

Madame Chermidy was quite determined on checking Germaine's recovery, but was too prudent to undertake anything at her own risk and peril. She knew that a crime is always a clumsy expedient, and her position was too fair for her to wish to risk it on the chance of a failure.

"You are right," Lump said to her ; "no crime! we must start on that understanding. A crime never profits the doer ; it only serves others. A rich man is killed on the highway, and the robbers find five shillings in his pockets ; the rest goes to the heirs."

"But in this case I am the heir."

"Of nothing, if we are caught in the act. Listen to me. In the first place, she may die of her own accord ; in the next place, if any one gives her a push along the road, we must not be mixed up in it."

"How is it to be done?"

"Make Germaine's death of interest to somebody. Suppose a sick man were to say to his servants, 'My lads, attend to me properly, and on the day of my death you will all have £50 a year.' Do you believe that such a man would have long to live? There would

be among the servants some intelligent fellow who
would carry out the doctor's prescriptions after his own
fashion.   He would receive his £50 a year, and the
heirs——"

" Would come into the property.   Then, we have
only to choose the servant; but suppose we stumble
on an honest man ?"

" Are there any ?"

" Lump, you calumniate human nature.   There are
many men who would not risk their necks for £50 a
year."

" Well! I am convinced that if we sent there a little
fellow such as I know—a true-born Parisian, spoiled
by the other servants, jealous of those he serves,—
envious of the luxury he witnesses—vicious as the
drains, he will have understood within a fortnight the
fortune offered him."

" Perhaps so ; but suppose he failed ?"

" Then take a man of experience : find a practitioner
who is accustomed to these matters, and makes a trade
of them."

" Lump, Lump, you are thinking of home."

" Well, there were some famous fellows at Toulon."

" Would you have me look for a servant in the
galleys ?"

" There are men who have served their time."

" Where are they to be found ?"

" Find out.   You can surely take so much trouble
to get the man you want."

A few hours after this conversation, Madame Chermidy—lovely as virtue—was doing the honours of

her drawing-room to some of the first gentlemen in Paris.

Among them was an old bachelor of most joyous temper, a first-rate talker and teller of anecdotes, and faithful to the old school of French gallantry. He was chief clerk in the Prefecture of Police.

Madame Chermidy herself handed him a cup of tea, which she sweetened with an ineffable smile. She talked for a long time with him, forced him to exhaust his stock of stories, and took the most lively interest in all he was kind enough to tell her. For the first time for many weeks she was unjust to other guests, and broke through her rule of rigid impartiality.

The excellent man was in the seventh heaven of delight, and shook the snuff off his frill with a visible satisfaction.

Still, as one must leave the best of company in the end, M. Dornet walked discreetly toward the door at a few minutes before twelve, while there were still some twenty guests in the room. But Madame Chermidy recalled him with the graceful boldness of a lady of the house, who does not pardon deserters.

"My dear M. Dornet," she said, "you have been so delightful that I cannot grant you your liberty at such an early hour. Come and sit by my side, and tell me another of your capital stories."

The excellent man willingly obeyed, although it was his principle to go to bed early and rise early; but he protested that she had emptied his budget, and unless he invented, he had nothing to tell. A few friends of the house formed a circle round him, to teaze him a

little, and keep him imprisoned. They asked him all
sorts of indiscreet questions; they wanted the truth
about the Iron Mask ; he was invited to name the
real author of Junius's letters, explain Gyges' ring,
the Council of Ten, and show the company some
Government scheme. He replied to all gaily and
quietly, with that smile of good temper which is the
fruit of a tranquil life. But he was not quite at his
ease, and fidgeted about in his chair, like a fish in a
frying-pan. Madame Chermidy, ever kind, came to
his aid, and said, " As I delivered you into the hands
of the Philistines, it is but just that I should liberate
you ; but on one condition."

" I accept with my eyes shut, madame."

" It is said that nearly all the crimes society suffers
from are committed by relapsed criminals—liberated
convicts—is not that the name given them ?"

" Yes, madame."

" Well, have the kindness to explain to us what a
liberated convict is."

The gentle clerk took off his spectacles, wiped them
with the corner of his handkerchief, and replaced them
on his nose. All the remaining guests collected round
him, and made ready to listen. The duke leaned
against the mantelpiece, little suspecting that he was
abetting in his daughter's murder. People of fashion
have a dainty curiosity, and the minor mysteries of
crime are a piquant meal for surfeited minds.

" Good gracious, madame," the Head of the Office
said, " if you only require a simple definition, I shall
yet get to bed at an early hour. Liberated convicts

are men who have served their time at the galleys. Allow me to kiss your hand, and to take leave."

" How, is that all ?"

" Absolutely ; and I may mention that I know more of the persons of whom you are speaking than, probably, any man in France. I never saw one of them, but I have all their descriptions in my books ; I know their past, their profession, their trade, their residence ; and I could tell you all their names: Christian names, false names, and nicknames."

" In the same way that Cæsar (as I may say in comparison) knew all the soldiers in his army."

" Cæsar, madame, was more than a great captain, he was the first clerk of his age."

" Were there any liberated convicts under the Roman Republic ?"

" No, madame ; and soon there will be none in France. We are beginning to follow the example of the English, who have substituted transportation for the hulks. Public security will gain by it, and the prosperity of ur colonies will not suffer. The galleys were the school of all vices : the transported become moral by labour."

" All the worse ! I regret the liberated convicts. It was so nice in the romances ! But tell me, M. Dornet, what do these people do? what do they say ? where do they live? how are they dressed? where can they be found ? how are they to be recognised ? are they still branded in the back ?"

" Some of them, the deans of the order The branding-iron was suppressed in 1791, re-established

in 1806, and definitively abolished by the law of
April 28, 1832. A liberated convict is in every
respect like an honest man. He dresses as he pleases,
and carries on the trade he has learned. Unfortunately
they have nearly all been apprenticed to robbery."

"But there are respectable men among them,
surely?"

"Not many. Think of the education of the galleys.
Besides, it is very difficult for them to earn an honest
livelihood."

"Why so?"

"Their antecedents are known, and masters do not
like to engage them; their fellow-workmen despise
them. If they have any money, and set up on their
own account, they cannot hire workmen."

"They are recognised, then, by what sign? If one
were to come and try to enter my service, how should
I know what he is?"

"There is no danger of that. They are not allowed
to live in Paris, because the surveillance would be too
difficult. They are assigned a residence in the provinces, in some small town, and the local police watch
them closely."

"And if they come to Paris without your permission?"

"They would break their leave, and we should
transport them by virtue of a law of December 8, 1851."

"But, in that case, there is no one left in the *tapis-
francs*?"

"The Municipal Council of the Department of the
Seine has destroyed the houses of which you speak.

There are no caves for the wild beasts, and no wild beasts for the caves."

"Good gracious! why, we are reaching a golden age, M. Dornet. You rob me of my illusions one by one. You render my life quite prosaic."

"Fair lady, life will never be prosaic to those who have the happiness of seeing you."

This compliment was so politely addressed, that all the company applauded. M. Dornet blushed up to the whites of his eyes, and looked at the points of his shoes; but Madame Chermidy soon brought him back to the point. "Where are there any liberated convicts?" she asked him. "Are there any at Vaugirard?"

"No, madame; there are none in the department of the Seine."

"At St. Germaine?"

"No."

"At Compiègne?"

"No."

"At Corbeil?"

"Yes."

"How many?"

"You expect, perhaps, to catch me tripping?"

"I am certain of it."

"Well, then, there are four."

"Their names? Come, Cæsar!"

"Nabichon, Lebrasseur, Chassepie, and Mantoux."

"Why, that is a verse."

"You have at once guessed the secret of my remembering them."

"Tell us that again. Nabichon——"

"Lebrasseur, Chassepie, and Mantoux."

"Well, that is curious. Now, we are all as clever as you. Nabichon, Lebrasseur, Chassepie, and Mantoux. And pray what do these honest gentlemen do?"

"The two first are temporarily in a paper-mill, the third is a gardener, the fourth keeps a blacksmith's shop."

"M. Dornet, you are a great man : pardon me for having doubted your learning."

"So long as you do not doubt my devotion."

M. Dornet took leave ; it was one in the morning, and all Madame Chermidy's guests rose one after the other. They kissed her little white hand, which was quivering with the hope of a successful crime. In replying to their adieux, the pretty woman repeated between her teeth poor Monsieur Dornet's verse: Nabichon, Lebrasseur, Chassepie, and Mantoux.

The Duke was the last to leave. "What are you thinking of?" he said to her ; "you are full of thought."

"I am thinking of Corfu."

"Better think of your friends in Paris."

"Good-night, my lord. I believe that Lump has found you a servant. She will make the proper inquiries, and we will speak about it again in a few days."

The next morning, Lump took the train for Corbeil. She stopped at the Hôtel de France, and remained in the town till Sunday. She visited the paper-mill, bought flowers of all the gardeners, and went about the streets a good deal. On the Sunday morning she lost the key of her carpet-bag, and she went to a little locksmith, who was blowing his forge in spite of the

law of Dominical rest. The sign bore the words,
" MANTOUX LITTLELUCK, *Locksmith in all its Branches.*"
The master was a little man of from thirty to thirty-
five years of age, brown, well made, sharp, and wide
awake. It was not necessary to look twice at him in
order to guess to what faith he belonged : he was of
those who keep their Sunday on a Saturday. The love
of gain glistened in his little black eyes, and his nose
resembled the beak of a bird of prey. Lump begged
him to come to the hotel and force a lock, and he performed his task in thorough style. Lump kept him by
her side through the charms of her conversation. She
asked him if he were satisfied with business, and he
replied like a man disgusted with life. Nothing had
succeeded with him since his birth. He had gone into
service as a groom, and his master had discharged
him. Then he was apprenticed to a locksmith, and
the susceptibility of some of the customers had caused
him grave misfortune. At twenty, he joined some
friends in a magnificent affair—a piece of lock-making
in which all the partners must gain their fortunes. In
spite of his zeal and skill, he had failed shamefully, and
it had taken him ten years to recover from his fall.
The name of *Littleluck* had adhered to him since that
period. He had come to set up at Corbeil, after a long
stay in the South. The authorities of the town knew
him well and took an interest in him : he received now
and then a visit from the Superintendent of Police.
But, for all that, he had no great amount of work to
do, and but few houses were open to him.

Lump pitied his misfortunes, and asked him why he

did not go and try his luck elsewhere. He answered, iu a melancholy voice, that he had neither the desire nor the means to travel. He was settled here for a long time. Where the goat is tied up, there it must browse.

" Even when there is nothing to browse ?" Lump asked.

He nodded as the only reply.

Lump said to him :—" If I have any skill in physiog-nomy, you are a worthy man as I am an honest woman. Why do you not go back into service, as you say you were a groom ?   I wait on a single lady in Paris, and might be able to find you a place."

" I thank you from my heart," he replied ; " but I am forbidden to reside in Paris."

" By your physician ?"

" Yes : my chest is delicate."

" Fortunately the situation is not at Paris. It is out of France, near Turkey, in a country where consump-tive people are cured by putting them out to be treated by the sun."

" I should like that much if the family were highly respectable.   But I should require a good many things to cross the frontier : money, papers, and so on, and I have nothing of all that."

" You would not be allowed to want for anything, if you suited my lady.   You must come and see her for an hour or two at Paris."

" Oh, that is possible.   Nothing would happen to me, even if I stayed a day with you."

" Of course not."

" If the matter could be arranged, I should like to

take another name in my passport. I have had enough
of mine; it has brought me nothing but ill-luck, and
I would leave it in France with my old clothes."

"You are quite right. That is what is called putting
on a new skin. I will mention you to my lady, and
if matters can be arranged, I will drop you a line."

Lump returned to Paris the same evening. Mantoux,
surnamed Littleluck, fancied he had met with a beneficent fairy under the form of a gigantic ape. Glorious visions collected round his bed : he dreamed that
he became at one stroke rich and honest, and that the
French Academy decreed him a prize of virtue of £2000
a-year. He received a letter on the Monday evening,
broke his ban, and arrived at Madame Chermidy's on
the Tuesday morning. He had shaved off his beard
and cut his hair, but Lump took very good care not to
ask the reason why.

The splendour of the house dazzled him ; the severe
dignity of Madame Chermidy imposed on him. The
fair criminal had assumed the countenance of a Lord
Chief Baron. She ordered him to her presence, and
asked him about his past life, like a woman who cannot
be deceived. He lied like a prospectus, and she took
care to believe him on his word. When he had supplied all the requisite explanations, she said to him :—

"My lad, the place I am about to give you is one of
confidence. A friend of mine, the Duke de la Tour, is
looking for a servant to wait on his daughter, who is
dying abroad. There will be good wages for a year or
two, and an annuity of £60 a-year on the death of the
young lady. She is given up by all the physicians in

Paris. The wages will be paid you by the family; but I will guarantee the annuity. Behave as a faithful servant, and await the end patiently; you will lose nothing by delay."

Mantoux swore by the God of his fathers that he would attend to the young lady like a sister, and compel her to live a hundred years.

"That is well," Madame Chermidy replied. "You will wait upon us this evening, and I will present you to the Duke. Show yourself to him in your true character, and I will answer that he engages you."

She added to herself, "Whatever may happen, the scamp will see in me his dupe, and not his accomplice."

Mantoux served at table, after taking a careful lesson from his stanch patroness, Lump. The guests were four in number; there were the same number of servants to change the plates, and the locksmith needed only to look on. Madame Chermidy had thought it as well to give him a lesson in toxicology, and had chosen her guests in consequence. They were a barrister, a professor of forensic medicine, and the Duke.

She very gently led the Doctor round to the subject of poisoning. Men who understand this delicate matter are generally chary of their science; but they forget themselves sometimes at table. A secret which a man is careful to hide from the public, may be told in confidence, when the audience consists of a barrister, a great gentleman, and a pretty woman of large fortune. Servants do not count; it is settled that they have no ears.

Unfortunately for Madame Chermidy, the poisons

came on before the champagne. The Doctor was prudent, gossiped a good deal, but did not betray himself. He retrenched himself in archæological curiosities, declared that the science of poisoning had not progressed, that we had lost the recipes of Locusta, Lucrezia Borgia, Catherine de Medici, and the Marchioness of Brinvilliers! He laughingly regretted the fine secrets lost, wept for the annihilating poison of young Britannicus, the perfumed gloves of Jeanne d'Albret, the powder of succession, and that household liqueur which converted Cyprus into Syracuse wine; nor did he forget a cursory remark on the fatal bouquet of Adrienne Lecouvreur. Madame Chermidy remarked that the young locksmith was listening with all his ears. "Tell us about modern poisons," she said to the doctor; "poisons employed in our day—poisons in active service."

"Unhappily, Madame," he replied, "we have fallen to a very low ebb. The difficulty is not to kill people, —a pistol-ball would settle the business; but to kill them without leaving a trace. Poison is of no use for anything else, and that is its only advantage over the pistol. But, so soon as a new poison is brought out, a means of proving its presence is discovered. The demon of Good has wings as long as the genius of Evil. Arsenic is a good workman, but Marsh's apparatus is there to control the work. Nicotine is by no means a foolish invention, strychnine is also highly to be recommended; but they have found their masters—in other words, their re-agents. Phosphorus was taken up with some show of reason. The argument was, that the human body contains large quantities of phos-

phorus; if the chymical analysis discovers it in the
body of the victim, I will reply that nature put it there.
But we have beaten down all these arguments. Of
course, there is no difficulty in killing people, but it is
almost impossible to do so with impunity. I could tell
you the means of poisoning four-and-twenty people at
once in a close room, without giving them anything
liquid. The experiment does not cost sixpence; but
the assassin would have to give his head in the bargain. A very talented chymist has recently invented
a subtile composition which possesses considerable
charms. By breaking the ball in which it is con-
tained, people will tumble off like flies. But you cannot persuade anybody that they died fairly."

"Doctor," Madame Chermidy asked, "what is Prussic acid?"

"Prussic acid, Madame, is a poison very difficult to
manufacture, impossible to purchase, and equally impossible to keep pure even in glass vessels."

"Does it leave traces?"

"Magnificent ones. It stains people blue: and thus
Prussian blue was discovered."

"You are laughing at us, doctor: you do not respect
the most sacred thing in the world—a woman's curiosity. I have heard of an American or African poison,
which kills people by the prick of a pin. Is that an
invention of the romancers?"

"No; it is an invention of the savages. It is used
on the barbs of arrows. It is a pretty poison; it does
not allow a man to languish; it is miniature lightning.
The most curious part of the thing is that it may be

eaten with impunity. The savages employ it in sauces and combats—in the field and in the kitchen."

"You have just told us its name, but I cannot call it to mind."

"I did not tell it you, Madame; but I am quite willing to do so. The *Curare*. It is sold in Africa, in the Mountains of the Moon. The merchants are anthropophagists."

Madame Chermidy had wasted her dinner. The Doctor carefully kept to himself the terrible stock-in-trade every physician carries with him. But the Duke was touched by Mantoux's assiduity and attention, and took him into his daughter's service.

CHAPTER VIII.

HAPPY DAYS.

In reading the history of the French Revolution, it causes no slight surprise to find in it months of profound peace and unclouded happiness. Passions slumber, animosities rest; parties walk onward like brothers hand in hand, and enemies embrace on the public squares. These happy days are like resting-places made from station to station on a blood-stained road.

Similar halting-places are found in the most agitated or most unhappy life. Revolutions of mind and body, passions, and diseases cannot go on without some moments of rest. Man is a being so weak that he can neither act nor suffer continuously; were he not to halt a little now and then, his strength would be prematurely exhausted.

The summer of 1853 was to Germaine one of those moments of rest which arrive so opportunely for human weakness. She took advantage of it—she enjoyed her nascent happiness, and collected a small measure of strength to support her in the trials through which she had still to pass.

The climate of the Ionian Islands is incomparably soft and regular. The winter is merely a transition from autumn to spring, and the summers grow almost wearisome through their unvaried serenity. From time to time a passing cloud will hurry over the Seven Islands, but does not stop; people have often to wait there three months for a drop of rain. In this arid paradise the natives do not say, " wearisome as rain," but " wearisome as fine weather."

The pure weather, however, did not weary Germaine : it cured her slowly. M. le Bris watched this miracle of the blue sky : he looked on while nature was acting, and followed with passionate interest the gradual pro. gress of a power superior to his own. He was too modest to claim the honour of the cure, and confessed in good faith that the only infallible medicine is that coming from on High.

Still, in order to deserve the aid of Heaven, he himself aided it a little. He had received from Paris Dr. Chartroul's iodometer, with a stock of iodized cigarettes. These cigarettes, composed of aromatic herbs and soothing plants infused in a tincture of iodine, introduce the medicament into the lungs, accustom those most delicate organs to the presence of a foreign body, and prepare the patient to inhale pure iodine through the tubes of the apparatus. Unfortunately the machine was found to be broken on arrival, although packed by the Duke himself and carried with great care by the new servant. Hence, a new one had to be ordered, and this took time.

After a month of this anodyne treatment, Germaine felt a sensible improvement. She was not so weak during the day, she endured the fatigue of a long walk more easily, and she did not so frequently seek refuge

on her couch. Her appetite was greater and decidedly
more permanent; she no longer rejected food after
tasting it; she ate, digested, and slept in good spirits;
the night-fever was much calmed, and the perspiration
which bathes all consumptive people in their sleep
daily decreased.

Her heart, also, gradually began to grow convalescent;
her despair, her savage temper, and hatred of those who
loved her, gave way to a gentle and benevolent melancholy. She was so happy at feeling herself regenerated,
that she wished to thank both Heaven and earth.

Convalescents are great children who cling to everything that surrounds them, through fear of falling.
Germaine kept her friends round her, for she feared
solitude; she wished to be encouraged every moment,
and would say to the Countess, " I am getting better,
am I not?' and added in a lower voice, " I shall not
die!" The Countess replied with a laugh, " If Death
were to come to fetch you, I would show him my face,
and he would run away." The Countess was proud of
her ugliness as other women are of their beauty, for
coquetry creeps in everywhere.

Don Diego waited patiently till Germaine turned to
him. He was too delicate and proud to importune her
with his attentions; but he was always within reach,
ready to take the first step so soon as she summoned
him by a glance. It soon grew with her a pleasant
custom to notice this discreet and silent friendship.
There was something heroic and grand in the Count's
ugliness, which women appreciate more than mere
good looks. He was not one of those men who make

conquests, but he could inspire a passion. His long swarthy face, his large bronze hands, formed a striking contrast to his white linen clothes. His large black eyes emitted beams of gentleness and goodness ; his powerful and ringing voice had at times sweetly-modulated inflections. In the end Germaine compared this grandee of Spain to a tamed lion.

When she walked in the garden amid the old orange-trees, or under the tamarisks on the shore, leaning on the arm of the Dowager, or with little Gomez hanging to her skirt, the Count followed her at a distance without any affectation, with a book in his hand. He did not put on the downcast look of a lover, or waft his sighs along the breeze ; he seemed like an indulgent father desirous to watch his children and yet not control their sports by his presence. His affection for his wife was a composite of Christian charity, compassion for weakness, and that bitter joy which a man of honour finds in the accomplishment of difficult duties. Perhaps, too, some degree of legitimate pride was blended with it. It is a glorious victory to snatch a certain prey from the clutches of death, and to create again a being whom illness had almost destroyed. Physicians understand that pleasure ; they grow attached to those whom they have brought back from the other world, and feel for them the tenderness of a creator to the creature.

Custom, which reconciles everything, had also brought Germaine to talk with her husband. When people are together from morning to night, hatred cannot ever endure between them ; they talk, they reply—for that

pledges them to nothing; but life is only possible at
that price.   She called him Don Diego; he addressed
her simply as Germaine.

One day (it was in the middle of June) she was lying
in the garden on a Turkey carpet.   The old Countess,
seated near her, was mechanically telling a rosary of
coral beads, while little Gomez was stuffing his pockets
with fallen oranges.   The Count passed ten paces off,
book in hand.   Germaine sat up, and invited him to
take a chair.   He obeyed without further pressure,
and put his book in his pocket.

"What were you reading?" she asked.

He replied, blushing like a schoolboy detected in a
fault, "You will laugh at me.   It is Greek."

"Greek!—you can read Greek! How could a man
like you amuse himself by learning Greek?"

"By the merest accident.   My tutor might have
been an ass like so many others, but he happened to be
a learned man."

"And you read Greek for amusement?"

"Homer, yes; I am in the middle of the *Odyssey*"

Germaine feigned a little yawn.   "I read a translation of that," she said; "there were a sword and a
helmet on the cover of the book."

"Then you would be much astonished were I to
read you Homer in the original; you would not recognise it."

"Much obliged, but I do not care for stories of
battles."

"There is nothing of the sort in the *Odyssey*.   It is
a romance of manners, the first ever written, and per-

haps the best. Our fashionable authors could invent
nothing more interesting than this history of a country
squire who leaves his home to earn money, comes back
after twenty years' absence, finds an army of scamps
installed in his house, coercing his wife and wasting
his property, and kills them with his arrows. The only
fault in this history is, that it has always been translated
for us with so much emphasis. The young rustics who
besieged Penelope have been converted into so many
kings; the farm is disguised as a palace, and gold is
plastered on everywhere. If I might venture to translate you a page, you would be amazed at the simple
and familiar truth of the narrative. You would see
with what amusing delight the poet talks of black wine
and succulent meat; how he admires closely-fitting
doors and well-planed boards. You would see, above
all, how exactly nature is described, and find in my
book the sea, the heaven, and the garden here before
you."

"You may try," Germaine said; "you will be able
to see when I have fallen asleep."

The Count willingly obeyed, and began translating
the first book. He rolled out before Germaine's eyes
that grand Homeric style which is richer, more varie-
gated, and more sparkling than the brilliant webs of
Beyrout or Damascus. His translation was the more
liberal because he did not understand every word, but
he understood the poet. He cut down long passages,
developed in his own fashion any that were curious,
and added an intelligent commentary to the text. In
short, he interested his beloved audience, always except-

ing the Marquis de los Montes, who roared in his desire to interrupt the reading. Children are like birds, when people are talking before them, they sing.

I cannot say if the young couple reached the end of the *Odyssey*, but Don Diego had found means to excite his wife's interest, and that was a good deal. It grew a habit with her to hear him read, and to feel comfortable in his society. She soon saw in him a superior mind, and although he was too timid to speak in his own name, the presence of a great poet gave him boldness, and his own ideas came to light under the protection of another's thoughts. Dante, Ariosto, Cervantes, and Shakspeare were the sublime mediators who undertook to bring these two minds together, and render them dear to each other. Germaine did not feel at all humiliated by her own ignorance and her husband's superiority, for a woman delights to be a nullity in comparison with the man she loves.

They formed a habit of living together and meeting in the garden to talk and read. It was not gaiety, but a certain calm and friendly serenity that formed the charm of these meetings. Don Diego knew not how to laugh, and his mother's laugh resembled a nervous grimace. The Doctor, though so frank and hearty, seemed to sing a false note when he flung his grain of sand into the conversation. Germaine still coughed at times, and that restless expression produced by the vicinity of death still remained on her countenance. And yet these cloudless summer days were the first happy hours of her youth.

How often, in the intimacy of this family life, the

Count's mind was troubled by the remembrance of Madame Chermidy no one ever knew, and I will not take it on myself to say. It is probable that solitude, listlessness, and the privation of those lively pleasures in which a man expends his superfluous energy—in a word, that sap of spring which rises to the forehead of a man as to the summit of trees—caused him more than once to regret the noble resolution he had formed. The Trappists who turn their backs on the world after enjoying it, find in their cells arms all in readiness against the temptations of the past—in fasting, prayer, and a dietary sufficiently mortifying to kill the old Adam. There is probably more merit in wrestling as Don Diego did, like a soldier disarmed. M. le Bris watched him closely, like a patient who must be kept from a relapse. He rarely spoke to him of Paris, never of Madame Chermidy; and when he read in a French journal that the *Naiad* was anchored off Ky-Tcheou in the Sea of Japan, to demand reparation for the insult offered the two French missionaries, he tore up the paper, lest even Captain Chermidy's name might be brought up.

There are, in the eastern lands, certain hours when the southern breeze intoxicates a man's senses more powerfully than the wine of Tinos drank under the name of Malvoisie ; the heart melts like wax, the will loses its elasticity, the mind grows weak. You try to think, but your ideas slip away from you like water through your fingers. You fetch a book, a good old friend ; you try to read, but your thoughts wander at the first lines ; your eyes begin to swim ; your eye-

lids open and shut, you cannot say why. In these
hours of half-sleep and gentle quietude our hearts
expand of themselves. The masculine virtues have a
cheap triumph when a sharp frost reddens the nose
and sears the ear, and the December wind contracts
the fibres of the flesh and the will. But when the
jasmines spread their searching perfume around, when
the flowers of the pomegranate rain on our head, and
white sails appear in the distant sea like Nereids—oh,
then! we must be very deaf and very blunt if we see
or hear aught but love!

Don Diego noticed one day that Germaine had improved. Her cheeks were fuller; the furrows on her
exquisite face were filling up; the sinister wrinkles
were being effaced. A healthier colour, a sunbeam of
good omen, coloured her lovely brow, and her golden
hair was no longer the crown of a dead girl.

He had been reading to her for a long time; fatigue
and sleep had fallen on her simultaneously; her head
had fallen back, and she lay motionless in the arms of
her easy chair. The Count was alone with her. He
laid his book on the ground, approached her gently,
knelt before the young girl, and advanced his lips to
kiss her forehead; but he was restrained by a feeling
of delicacy. For the first time he thought with horror
of the way in which he had become Germaine's husband; he was ashamed of his bargain; he confessed to
himself that a kiss obtained by surprise would be
almost a crime, and he refrained from loving his wife
till the day that he was sure of being loved in return.

The party at the Villa Dandolo did not live in such

an abstract solitude as might be supposed. Isolation can only be found in large cities, where each lives for himself without taking any thought about his neighbours. In the country, the most indifferent persons form acquaintances ; man knows that he is born for society, and seeks the conversation of his fellow-mortals.

Few days passed without Germaine receiving some visitors. At first they came from curiosity, then through kindly interest, and lastly through friendship. This nook of the island was inhabited the whole year through by five or six modest families, who would have been poor in the town, and who wanted for nothing on their estates, because they could content themselves with little. Their houses fell into ruins, because they had not money to repair them ; but they carefully kept up over the entrance an escutcheon coeval with the Crusades. The Ionian Islands are the Hampton Court Palace of the East : you find there great virtues, and the minor wretchedness of aristocracy, pride, dignity, decent and onerous poverty, and a certain degree of elegance even amid the most scanty circumstances.

The owner of the villa, Count Dandolo, would not be disavowed by the doges, his ancestors. He is a little, quick, and intelligent man, well up in political affairs, vacillating between the Greek party and English influence ; but inclined to opposition, and ever ready to judge severely the acts of the Lord High Commissioner. He follows closely the old and new intrigues dividing Europe, watches the progress of the

British Lion, discusses the Eastern question, is alarmed
at the influence of the Jesuits, and is President of the
Corfu Freemasons. He is an excellent man, who takes
more time in navigating round a glass of water than an
East India trader in its passage. His son Spiro, a
handsome young man of thirty, has been gained over
to English ideas, like the whole of the younger generation; he associates with the officers, and is often seen
in their box at the theatre. The Dandolos could live
grandly if they could manage to sell their estates; but
in Corfu the inhabitants are as poor as the land is
rich. Every one is ready to sell, but no one ever
dreams of buying. The Count and Spiro speak
fluently the three languages of the Island—English,
Greek, and Italian : they know French in addition,
and their friendship was precious to Germaine. Spiro
interested himself in the fair invalid with all the
warmth of an unoccupied heart.

At times he brought with him a friend of his, Dr.
Delviniotis, Professor of Chemistry at the Corfu College.
He had formed a friendship for the invalid, which was
the more lively, because he had a daughter of her own
age. He gave M. le Bris the benefit of his advice,
talked with the dowager and the Count in Italian, and
was miserable because he could not speak French and
improve his acquaintance with Germaine. He might
be seen sitting before her for hours, studying a sentence,
or looking at her without uttering a word, with that
quiet and dumb politeness which prevails through the
whole of the East.

The most noisy man of the party was Captain Brétignières, an old Frenchman settled in Corfu since 1841. He had retired from service at the age of twenty-four with a pension and a wooden leg. This thin, bony gentleman would limp three miles to dine at the Villa Dandolo, when he told campaigning stories, twisted his moustache, and asserted that the Ionian Isles ought to belong to France. His gaiety affected the whole house. While draining his glass he would say, in a sententious voice : " When people esteem and love each other, they can drink as much as they like without injuring themselves." Germaine always dined with a good appetite when he was present; for this pleasant cripple, who clung so obstinately to life, dazzled her with a sweet hope, and forced her to believe that happiness yet awaited her. He played with the little Marquis, called him General, and rode him on his knee ; he gallantly kissed the invalid's hands, and waited on her with the devotion of an old page or a retired troubadour.

She had an admirer of a different school in the person of Mr. Stevens, Judge of the Royal Court of Corfu. This honourable magistrate spent his salary of one thousand pounds a year solely in taking care of his body. You never saw a man so clean, plump, and shiny, or health more calm and better stuffed. Egotistic, like all old bachelors ; serious, like all magistrates ; phlegmatic, like all Englishmen,—he concealed within the comfortable rotundity of his person a certain tinge of sensibility. Health appeared to him so precious a gift that he would have liked to impart it to the whole world. He had known the young English-

man we saw at Pompeii, and followed closely the
various phases of his recovery. He stated with great
simplicity that he had felt but little sympathy for this
pallid and dying little fellow ; but loved him more
every day as he saw him returning to life. He became
his intimate friend on the day that he could squeeze
his hand without forcing him to utter a cry of pain.
The same was the history of his acquaintance with
Germaine : he refrained from attaching himself to her
so long as he believed her condemned to death ; but
from the moment she seemed to take a place in the
world, he opened the folding-doors of his heart to
her.

The nearest neighbours of the family were Madame
Vitré and her son, and they soon became the most
intimate friends. The Baroness de Vitré had sought
shelter, with the remains of her fortune, at Corfu ; and
as she refrained from telling the story of her life, no one
ever knew what events drove her so far from her native
country. But one thing was evident at a glance, that
she had lived as an honourable woman, and educated her
son admirably. She was forty years of age, and had a
degree of beauty far from common ; but she busied
herself with her household and her dear Gaston with a
a methodic activity and unembarrassed zeal which
revealed her blood. True greatness is a gift which is
displayed in all the situations of life, and on every
stage ; it is shown both in toil and in repose, and it is
as brilliant in a farmyard as in a salon. Madame de
Vitré between her two servants, and dressed like
them in the national costume, resembled Penelope

embroidering the tunics of young Telemachus. Gaston de Vitré, fair as a young girl of twenty, led the rude and active life of a country gentleman. He worked with his own hands : felled the trees, and collected the harvest from the orange-trees and the pomegranates. In the morning he went out with his gun to shoot becaficos and ortolans ; in the evening he read with his mother, who was his professor and nursing mother of his mind. Without care for the future, ignorant of all worldly matters, and restricting his thoughts to the horizon that surrounded him, he could imagine no greater pleasure than a good day's sport, a new book, or a sail on the sea. He had a virgin heart, pure and white as a sheet of paper that woos the pen to write on it. When his mother brought him to the Villa Dandolo, he perceived for the first time that he was a little ignorant ; he blushed for the idleness in which he had lived, and regretted that he had not studied medicine.

Visits are always long in the country ; you have to go so far to pay them, that you are in no hurry to leave again. The Dandolos, the Vitrés, Dr. Delviniotis, the Judge, and the Captain often spent the whole day by the side of the lovely convalescent. She kept them there gladly, without explaining to herself the secret motive that caused her to do so. Already she began to avoid being alone with her husband ; for in the same proportion as declared love shuns intruders, and seeks *tête-à-têtes*, nascent love seeks a crowd and distractions. As soon as we begin to feel ourselves possessed by thoughts of another, strangers and indifferent persons seem to protect us against our own weakness; and we feel that we should be defenceless were they no longer there.

The dowager, without knowing it, aided this secret desire of Germaine's, for she kept Madame Vitré with her, whom she liked more and more every day. Don Diego had not yet reached that point where a lover endures with impatience the company of strangers; his affection for Germaine was still disinterested, because it was cold and calm. He sought before all else everything that would amuse his young wife, and attach her gently to existence. Perhaps, too, this timid man, like all men who are really strong, avoided explaining to himself the new feeling that attracted him towards her. He feared to find himself caught between two opposing duties, and he could not hide from himself that he was pledged for life to Madame Chermidy. He believed her worthy of his love; and he esteemed her, in spite of her error, as we all esteem a woman, innocent or guilty, of whose love we are secure. Had any man come, proof in hand, to tell him that Madame Chermidy was not worthy of him, he would have experienced a feeling of agony, and not of deliverance. It is not easy to break off from three years of happiness; and a man does not rub his hands and say, "Thank Heaven, my son is the child of a profligate woman!"

The count, then, experienced a moral discomfort, a sort of dull uneasiness, which ran counter to his rising passion. He feared to read himself, and he stood before his heart as if before a letter of which he dared not break the seal.

In the meanwhile the young couple sought each other, and felt happy, and in their hearts thanked the persons who prevented them from being alone together. The circle of friends that collected round them sheltered their love, just as the great elms that surround the Normandy orchards protect the delicate blossom of the apple-trees.

The receiving-room was in the middle of the garden. Germaine, seated in her easy chair, smoked iodized cigars ; the Count watched her enjoyment of life ; while the Dowager played with the child like a tall old black Faun with her tanned babe. The friends sat around in American rocking-chairs ; while Mantoux, or some other footman, served coffee, ices and sweetmeats, according to the usages of Eastern hospitality. The visitors were rather surprised that the mistress of the house was the only smoker in the whole company, for people smoke everywhere in the East. You throw away your cigarette at the door, but the mistress of the house offers you another while welcoming you. Germaine, either because she was inclined to indulge her husband's fault, or because she took pity on the poor Greeks, who could not live without tobacco, one day decreed that the cigarette would henceforth be permitted throughout her entire empire ; and when Don Diego smilingly reminded her of her old repugnance, she blushed, and quickly replied : " I have read in *Monte Cristo* that Turkish tobacco was a perfume, and as I know that no other is smoked here in sight of the shores of Turkey, there is no question about your odious cigars, the very sight of which makes me ill."

Before long, the grand chibouk, with red bowl and amber mouthpiece, and the nargiléh, which "singeth a pleasant tune" in smoking, made their appearance in the garden and the house. At the end of July, the odious cigars timidly escaped from some invisible receptacle, and found mercy in Germaine's sight. This was a sign that she was much better.

It was about this period that the elect of Madame Chermidy, Mantoux, called *Littleluck*, decided on poisoning his mistress.

There is some good in the most vicious man, and I am bound to confess that Mantoux was an excellent servant for two months. When the duke, who was ignorant of his history, procured him a passport in the name of Mathieu, he crossed the frontier joyfully and gratefully. Perhaps he really dreamed of being an honest man. Germaine's gentleness, the charm she threw over all those who came near her, the excellent wages she paid her people, and the slight hope entertained of saving her, inspired this contraband valet with honest feelings. He knew better how to pick a lock than to prepare a glass of sugar-water, but he strove not to appear a novice, and succeeded. He belonged to an intelligent race, fit for anything, skilful in all trades even in all arts. He applied himself so well, made such progress, and learnt his duties in so short a time, that his masters were satisfied with him.

Madame Chermidy had recommended him to conceal his religion, and deny it, even if cross-questioned ; for she knew how intolerant Spaniards of old blood are toward Israelites. Unfortunately this honest man could not hide his face, and Madame de Villanera suspected him of being at least a converted Hebrew. Now, as a good Spaniard, she drew little distinction between converts and heretics : she was the best woman in the world, and yet would have sent them all to the stake pell-mell, feeling assured that the twelve Apostles would have done the same.

Mantoux, who had more than once compromised with his conscience, felt no scruples in denying the religion of his fathers. He even consented to hear mass with the other servants ; but through one of those contradictions of which man is full, he could never make up his mind to eat the same meat as his comrades. Without drawing attention to his repugnance, he ate vegetables, fruit, and salads, like an ardent vegetarian. He consoled himself for this lenten fare when sent on an errand to town ; then he ran straight to the Jew quarter, fraternised with his people, talked that same Hebrew which serves as a bond to the great dispersed nation, and ate *kaucher* meat—that is to say, killed by the sacrificer according to the precepts of the law. This was a consolation he must have missed sadly at the period when he resided in the galleys.

In conversing with his co-religionists, he learned a good many things : that Corfu was an excellent country, a real Promised Land, where living was remarkably cheap, and a man was rich with sixty pounds a-year. He learned that English justice was severe, but that with a good boat and two oars it was possible to escape the clutches of the law. It was merely necessary to steer for Turkey : the continent was only a few miles off ; he could see it, almost touch it ! Last of all, he learned where arsenic could be bought at the fairest prices.

Toward the end of July he heard several persons affirm that the young Countess was on a fair way to recover : he assured himself of it with his own eyes, and expected to see her recovery every day. On handing her a glass of sugared water each evening, he noticed with Dr. le Bris the decrease of the cough and the diminution of the fever. He was present one day at the unpacking of a box much better packed than the one he had brought from Paris. He saw a charming apparatus of copper and glass taken out of it, a remarkably simple machine, so appetizing that the mere sight of it made one regret not being consumptive. The Doctor hastened to put it up, and said, as he regarded it tenderly, "perhaps this will prove the Countess's salvation."

This remark was the more painful to Mantoux, because he had just formed a design to buy a delicious little property close by, a perfect nest for honest people. The idea occurred to him of breaking this engine of destruction which threatened his future fortune ; but he thought that he should be discharged if he did so, and lose his wages as well as his pension. Hence he resigned himself to be merely a faithful servant.

Unluckily, his companions talked loudly about his vegetable diet ; the Dowager was alarmed, inquired into matters, and decided that he was an incorrigible

Jew relapsed, and all that follows. She asked him if he would prefer looking for a place in Corfu or returning to France. In vain did he beg for mercy and seek the charitable intervention of kind-hearted Germaine, for the Dowager would not listen to reason in such an affair as this. All that he obtained was, that he should keep his place till his successor arrived.

He had a month before him, and this is how he profited by it. He procured some arsenious acid and concealed it in his bedroom. He took a pinch of it, about a dose for two men, and dissolved it in a large glass of water. He placed this glass in the pantry on a tall shelf which could only be reached by standing on a chair, and, without loss of time, poured several drops of this poisoned liquid into the invalid's sugared water. He decided on doing this daily, killing his mistress by slow degrees, and thus deserving Madame Chermidy's benefaction—in spite of the little apparatus.

CHAPTER IX.

LETTERS FROM CHINA AND PARIS.

*To Monsieur Mathieu Mantoux, at the Count de Villa-
nera's, Villa Dandolo, Corfu.*

No date.

" You do not know me, but I know you as well as if
I had made you. You are an ex-scholar of the Government Naval School at Toulon ; it was there I saw you
for the first time. I met you afterwards at Corbeil ;
you were not doing very brilliantly, and the police had
their eyes upon you. You had the luck to fall in with
a great fool of a Parisian who got you a good place,
with the hope of a pension. The lady and her maid
take you for a servant. I hear that your masters
honour you with their confidence. If the patient you
wait on had taken a passage to the other world, you
would be rich, respected, and live like a gentleman in
any country you please. Unfortunately, she has not
made up her mind to it, and you have not had the
sense to push her along the road. All the worse for
you ; you will keep your name of *Littleluck.* The
Inspector of Police at Corbeil is looking after you, and
is on the trail. If you do not take care you will be
found out, just as I, who am writing to you, found
you. Would you like to go and pick pepper in Cayenne ?
To work, then, sluggard ; fortune is in your hands, so

surely as my name is—— But you have no need to know my name. I am not Nabichon, or Lebrasseur, or Chassepie; but I am, in the hope that you will understand your interests, your friend.

"X. Y. Z."

Madame Chermidy to Dr. le Bris.

Paris, Aug. 13, 1853.

"Key of Hearts, my delightful friend, I have most magnificent news for you. Madame de Sévigné would make you wait for it for a couple of pages; but I go to work more quickly, and tell you at once. I am a widow, my dear friend, a widow without appeal, a widow by law. I have received the official notification, the burial certificate, the compliments of condolence from the ministry of Marine, the sword and epaulettes of the defunct, and a pension of thirty pounds to keep my carriage with in my old days. Widow! widow! widow! There is not a prettier word in the language. I have dressed myself in black. I walk about the streets, and feel inclined to stop the passers-by to tell them I am a widow.

"I discovered on this occasion that I was no ordinary woman. I know more than one who would have wept through human weakness, and to give some slight satisfaction to his manes; but I laughed like a madwoman, and rolled on Lump, who was just as bad as I was. Chermidy is no more. Chermidy is gone, as clean as the palm of my hand. I am justified in calling him the late Chermidy.

"You know, Tomb of Secrets, that I never loved that man, and that he was nothing to me. I bore his name,

and I endured his abuse ; two or three blows he gave
me were the sole ties love had formed between us.
The only man I ever loved, my real husband, my real
spouse before God, was never called Chermidy.   My
fortune does not come from that sailor; I owe him
nothing, and I should be a hypocrite if I mourned for
him.   Were you not present at our last interview ?
Do you remember the conjugal grimace that improved
his features ?   If you had not been present, he would
have played me an ill-turn.   Those sea-monsters are
capable of anything.   The cards have often told me
that I should die a violent death ; probably they knew
Chermidy.   He would have wrung my neck, sooner
or later, and danced at my funeral.   Now it is my turn
to laugh and dance.

"The history of his death, on my word, is famous ;
you never saw such a thorough Chinese picture, and
I intend to have it painted on a screen.   All my friends
came yesterday to condole with me.   They had prepared mournful faces, but I told them the story, and
presto ! they all changed, as if by magic.   We never
left off laughing till half after twelve at night.

"Just imagine, my dear Doctor, that the *Naiad* was
anchored off Ky-Tcheou.   I have not been able to find
the place on any map, and I am in a state of despair.
The geographers of the present day are surely not up
to their work.   Ky-Tcheou ought to be in the Corean
Peninsula, in the Sea of Japan.   I have found Kiu-
Tcheou, but that is in the province of Ching-King, on
the Gulf of Leou-Tung, in the Yellow Sea.   Put yourself in the place of a poor widow who does not know

in what degree of latitude she was deprived of her husband.

"However this may be, the magistrates of Ky-Tcheou, or Kiu-Tcheou, at the mouth of the Li-Kiang river, had ill-treated two French missionaries. The mandarin, governor, or father of the family, the powerful Gou-Ly, employed all his leisure hours in sending strangers to a happier world. There are three European factories at this pleasant spot, and a French silk-buyer performed the duties of consular agent. He had a flag before his door, and the missionaries lodged with him.   Gou-Ly sent to arrest the two priests, and accused them of preaching a strange religion.   They could not deny it with good grace, for they had come precisely for that purpose : they were condemned, and the report spread that they had been put to death. Under these circumstances the Admiral sent the *Naiad* up to see what was going on, and the commander ordered Gou-Ly on board.   You can imagine my husband *tête-à-tête* with this Chinese.   Gou-Ly protested that the missionaries were perfectly well, but that they had infringed the laws of the country, and must remain six weeks in prison.   My husband asked to see them, and it was proposed to show them to him behind the bars.   He went that same evening to the prison with a company of marines ; he saw two missionaries in ecclesiastical robes gesticulating at the window. The French consul recognised them, and everybody was satisfied.

"The next day, however, the consul was told that the missionaries had been really strangled a week before the arrival of the *Naiad*, and twenty witnesses were heard, who verified to the fact. My husband put on his uniform, landed his men, returned to the prison and broke in the doors, in spite of the signs of the missionaries, who moved their arms about to make him go back to the ship. He found in the dungeon two wax images modelled with Chinese perfection; they were the missionaries shown him on the previous evening.

"My husband got into a furious passion, for he did not like being deceived ; that was a fault I always had to find with him. He went back on board, and swore his great oath that he would bombard the town if the murderers were not punished. The mandarin, trembling like a leaf, made his submission, and condemned the judges to be sawn asunder between planks. Of course my husband could say nothing against that.

"But the legislature of the country permits any person condemned to death to supply a substitute. There are special agencies which, for a sum of two to three hundred pounds and fine promises, induce a poor devil to let himself be sawn in pieces. The Chinese of the lower classes, who grovel pell-mell with the animals, do not hold enormously to life, so they will willingly consent to have a short life and a merry one when they are offered a thousand dollars to squander in three days. My husband accepted the substitutes— was present at the punishment, and made his peace with the ingenious Gou-Ly. He carried his clemency to such an extent as to invite him to dinner the next day, with the magistrates whose lives had been bought off. This was acting like a clever diplomatist ; for, after all, what is diplomacy? the act of pardoning

insults, as soon as you have obtained entire satisfaction
for them.

"Gou-Ly and his accomplices went to dine in great
state on board the *Naiad*. The dessert was interrupted
by a magnificent fire ; the vessel flared like a lucifer-
match. The pumps were set to work just in time :
the accident was put upon a cook's mate, and apologies
were offered to the venerable Gou-Ly.

"Perhaps you may think the story rather long,—
but patience, you have not much longer to wait. The
mandarin would not be beaten in politeness, so he
invited the Captain the next day to one of those ban-
quets where Chinese prodigality triumphs. We are
but poor dumps by the side of those originals. The
gentleman who ate a twenty-pound dinner all to himself at the Café de Paris was greatly admired ; but the
Chinese would consider it a trifle. The commander
was promised ragouts powdered with fine pearls,
swallows' nests with golden pheasants' tongues, and
that celebrated omelette of peacocks' eggs which is
made on the table by killing the hens to obtain the
eggs. My Chermidy, who was as simple as an oar, did
not suspect that he would have to pay the bill. He
licked his lips, so the official report states, and promised
to listen with all his ears to the plays which season a
Chinese festival.

"He went on shore with the Consul and four men
as an escort, through a refreshing shower. You will
suppose that he had not forgotten his best uniform.
A deputation of magistrates received him at the landing-place with all the requisite ceremonies, and I

presume he was not dissatisfied with the harangue; for if the Chinese adore compliments, sailors do not detest them. He was mounted on a little pony. I think I can see him trotting along. The animal (I mean the pony) was sunk in the mud up to the knees, for the Chinese towns are paved with a macadam used for two modes of locomotion—carriages and boats. Twelve young men, dressed in rose-coloured silk, walked on his right and left, with peacocks' feathers in their hands. They sung through their noses the praises of the great, the powerful, the invincible Chermidy, and gently tickled his steed with the quills of their feathers. The little ones teased its nostrils, the taller boys the inside of its ears, until at last the animal reared. The rider, clumsy as a sailor, fell on his back, the boys ran up to him, and asked him all together if he had hurt himself? —if he wanted anything?—if he would have some water to wash, or like some smelling salts?—and while speaking, they drew their little knives from their pockets, and cut his throat without any noise or scandal, till the head was completely severed from the body.

" It was the Consul who told the story, and I really fear would not have told it, had it not been for the aid of the four sailors who saved his life, and took him back on board. I stop here; the piece is no longer interesting from the moment the hero is interred. You will know the rest from the newspapers and the enclosed letter, which the officers of the *Naiad* took the trouble to write to me. I sincerely regret the death of Mandarin Gou-Ly; were he still living, I would settle on him a pension of swallows' nests for the remainder of his life. As my happiness depends on a

double widowhood, I made a vow to divide fifty thousand pounds between the charitable souls who delivered
me from my enemies.   There were twenty-five thousand pounds in my secretaire for that mandarin who
does not live to enjoy them.

" Tomb of Secrets, you will burn my letters, I am
sure.   Burn, also, the newspapers which mention the
affair.   Don Diego must not learn that I am free, so
long as he is himself enchained.   Let us spare our
enemies too cruel regrets.   Above all, do not tell him
that I look remarkably well in black.

" Take great care of the person to whom you are
devoted ; whatever may happen, you will have the
merit of having made her live beyond all hope.   If you
had been told that you were leaving Paris for seven or
eight months, would you be enjoying your becaficos so
much ?   When she is cured, or the other thing, you
will return to Paris, and we will get you a practice
together again, for I am sure that none of your patients
except myself will recognise you.

" The Duke de la Tour, who does me the honour of
dining at my table sometimes, has asked me to find
you another footman.   I did not inquire sufficiently
into the character of the first I sent you, and I lately
heard that he is a dangerous person.   So kick him out
as soon as possible, or keep him on your own respon-
sibility, until the arrival of his successor.

" Farewell, Key of Hearts.   My heart has been open
to you for a long time ; and if you are not the best of
all my friends, it is not my fault.   Take care of my
husband and my son, and I will be for life ever yours,

" HONORINE."

The Officers of the ' Naiad' to Madame Chermidy.

"Honkong, April 2, 1853.

"MADAME—The officers serving on board the *Naiad* fulfil a painful duty in adding their regrets to the grief which the loss of Commander Chermidy will cause you.

"An odious treachery has robbed France of one of her most honourable and experienced officers—you, madame, of a husband whose goodness and gentleness every one would appreciate ; and us of a chief, or rather a comrade, who made it a point of honour to lighten our duties by taking the greater portion on himself.

"The pleasure of revenge is but a weak consolation, madame, to a sorrow like yours. Still, we are proud of being able to tell you that we gave our brave commander a glorious funeral. When the Consul and the four sailors who were witnesses to the crime brought us the news on board, the senior lieutenant, who succeeded the excellent officer we had lost, ordered the factories to be evacuated ; and we then bombarded the town, and reduced it to ashes in two days. Gou-Ly and his accomplices believed themselves in safety in the fortress ; but a company of marines besieged them for a week with a couple of guns we landed. The *Naiad* did not return to her station till she had taken ample satisfaction for her commander. At this moment, madame, no town exists under the name of Ky-Tcheou. There is only a pile of ashes, which may be called the tomb of Commander Chermidy."

✳ ✳ ✳ ✳ ✳ ✳

CHAPTER X.

THE CRISIS.

THE most happy period in the life of a maiden is the year preceding her marriage. Any woman who takes the trouble to invoke her recollections, will see once more with a feeling of regret, that winter, blessed before all others, when her choice was made, but not known by the world. A crowd of timid and hesitating suitors pressed around her, disputed her bouquet and her fan, and spread around her an atmosphere of love which she inhaled with delight. She had distinguished among the crowd the man to whom she wished to give her hand; she had promised him nothing; she experienced a sort of joy in treating him like the rest, and hiding from him her preference. She felt a pleasure in making him doubt his happiness, or causing him to alternate between hope and fear, and in trying him a little every evening. But in her heart she immolated all her rivals to him, and laid at his feet all the homage she feigned to accept. She promised to herself to repay richly so much perseverance and resignation; and, above all, she enjoyed that eminently feminine pleasure of commanding all and obeying one man.

This triumphant period had been missing in Germaine's life; the year preceding her marriage had been

the most sorrowful and miserable of her poor youth.
But the year that followed brought some compensa-
tion : she lived at Corfu, in a circle of passionate admirers. All who approached her, both young and old,
felt for her a sentiment akin to love. She bore on her
fair brow that sign of melancholy which tells the whole
world that a woman is not happy, and that is an attraction which men cannot resist. The most daring fear
to offer themselves to a woman who appears to want
for nothing, but sorrow emboldens the most timid, and
every one strives to console the mourner. Physicians
were not wanting to minister to this mind diseased ;
young Dandolo, one of the most brilliant men in the
Seven Islands, was constantly at her side, dazzled her
by his talent, and imposed on her his haughty friendship with the authority of a man who is always successful. Gaston de Vitré displayed a restless solicitude for
her ; the boy felt himself awaking to a new life. He
had made no change in his habits ; his toil and his
pleasures went on as before ; but, when he read by his
mother's side, he saw suns shining in the pages of the
book ; he stopped, as if dazzled, in the midst of his
reading, and he would dream about verses which had
never struck him before. The kiss he gave his mother
at night burnt her forehead, and when he prayed, with
his head resting on the side of the bed, he saw strange
images pass between his eyes and his eyelids.

He could not sleep soundly as he used to do, he was
agitated and tortured by dreams. He rose long before
daybreak, and hurried into the country with feverish
impatience. His gun was lighter on his shoulder, and

his feet passed more rapidly over the dried herbage.
He ventured further out to sea, and his arms, grown
more robust, took delight in rowing; but whatever
might be the object of his life, an invisible charm
brought him every day into the vicinity of Germaine.
He turned towards her like the needle to the polar
star, unconscious of the power that attracted him.
She greeted him as a friend, and did not conceal the
pleasure she felt in seeing him; but he was ever in a
hurry to depart, or only entered as he passed, for his
mother was expecting him, and he would hardly sit
down. But the setting sun still found him near the
dear convalescent, and he was astonished to see that
the days were so short in the months of Autumn.

M. Stevens, that stout and worthy gentleman,
marked the time behind Germaine's chair, like a regiment of infantry; he showed her those thoughtful and
measured attentions which are the strong point of
men of fifty. He brought her bonbons, and told her
stories, and he lavished on her those little attentions
to which a woman is never insensible. Germaine did
not despise this kind coarse friendship, paternal in
form, but not so paternal as that of Dr. Delviniotis.
She also rewarded with a glance of kindness Captain Brétignières, that excellent man, who only
wanted a feather-bed to walk on; she delighted
to see him moving around her with all the noise
of a charge of horse. She felt a very tender
friendship for Dr. le Bris, and the little man, accustomed to pay innocent court to all his female patients,
did not exactly know how he felt towards the Countess

Villanera.   She changed before his face, and this new-born beauty might carry in a moment the fragile barrier separating friendship from love.

All these feelings badly described, and more difficult to name than to describe, caused the joy of the house and the happiness of Germaine.   She found a great difference between her last winter in Paris and her first summer in Corfu; the garden and the villa exhaled gaiety, hope, and love.   All the guests rivalled each other in wit and good humour, and Germaine felt herself regenerated by the gentle warmth of all these devoted hearts that beat for her.   If she took care to fan the flame by a little innocent coquetry, it was only because she wished to insure the conquest of her husband.

The painful reminiscences of her marriage had become gradually effaced from her memory.   She had forgotten the gloomy midnight marriage, and regarded herself as a bride whose presence is awaited in order to proceed to church.   She no longer thought of Madame Chermidy ; she no longer felt that internal shudder produced by the war of a rival.   Her husband appeared to her like a new man ; she believed herself a new woman, born yesterday : for was it not being born a second time to escape from certain death ?   She dated her birth back to the spring, and would say with a smile, "I am an infant four months old."   The old Countess confirmed her in this idea, by lifting her in her arms like a little child.

The presence of the Marquis should have reminded her of the reality, for it was difficult to forget that this child had a mother, who might come some day or other to reclaim the happiness of which she had been robbed. But Germaine was accustomed to regard the little Gomez as her son ; for maternal love is so innate in woman that it is developed long before marriage. Little children of two years of age may be seen offering a doll the breast. The Marquis was Germaine's doll ; she neglected herself to take care of her boy, and she had even grown to consider him a beauty, which proves that she had a real mother's heart. Don Diego regarded her with pleasure when she pressed to her heart this little tawny Gomez, for he was glad to see that the hereditary grimace of the Villaneras no longer terrified his wife.

Every evening at nine, the family and the servants assembled in the sitting-room to prayers, for the old Countess was much attached to this religious and aristocratic custom. She read the orisons herself in Latin. The Greek domestics readily joined in the Common Office, in spite of the schism which keeps them apart from the Latin Christians, and Mathieu Mantoux knelt in a dark corner, where he could see everything without being seen, and strove to trace the ravages of the arsenic in Germaine's face.

He had not once omitted to poison the glass of water he gave her every night, and he hoped that the arsenic taken in small doses would accelerate the progress of the illness, without leaving any visible traces. This is a prejudice very common among the lower classes ; they believe in the action of slow poisons. Master Mantoux, rightly surnamed *Littleluck*, could not know that poison kills people at once or not at all. He believed that particles of arsenic taken into the body would join together and form grains, but he forgot the indefatigable toil of nature, which constantly repairs all internal disorders. Had he taken a better lesson in toxicology, or remembered the example of Mithridates, he would have known that microscopic poisonings produce a very different effect from what he expected. But Mathieu Mantoux had not studied history.

He would have been even more astonished at hearing that arsenic, absorbed in small doses, is a remedy against consumption, and though it does not always cure, it produces great alleviation to the patient. The particles of poison burn in the lungs through coming in contact with the external air, and produce a factitious respiration. It is something to breathe freely, and Germaine was fully aware of the fact. Arsenic removes the fever, improves the appetite, facilitates sleep, and puts flesh on the bones; it does not injure the effect of other remedies, and sometimes aids them.

M. le Bris had often thought of treating Germaine by this method, but a very natural scruple had bidden him pause—he was not certain of saving the patient, and the confounded arsenic reminded him of Madame Chermidy. Mantoux, a doctor of less timidity, accelerated the effect of the iodine and Germaine's recovery.

Germaine had been inhaling iodine from the 1st of August to the 1st of September. The Doctor was present at each inhalation, and M. Delviniotis was often by his side. This mode of treatment is not infallible, but it is gentle and easy. A current of heated air slowly dissolves a small quantity of iodine, and bears it without effort or pain into the lungs. Pure iodine does not intoxicate sick persons like the tincture, nor does it parch the mouth like iodhydric ether, or produce coughing. Its only defect is leaving in the mouth a slight taste of rust, to which you soon grow accustomed.

The doctors gradually paved the way for this new application : in her impatience, Germaine would have risked anything, so that she might get well ; but they only allowed her an inhalation once a day of about five minutes. With time they increased the dose, and in proportion as the cure progressed, so did the quantity of iodine inhaled.

The cure went on with incredible rapidity, thanks to the discreet assistance of Mantoux, and a stranger presented at the Villa Dandolo would not have guessed there was an invalid in the house. At the end of August, Germaine was as fresh as a flower, plump as a peach. In this glorious garden, where Nature had accumulated all her marvels, the sun surveyed nothing more brilliant than this young woman, who came forth from her illness all fresh, like a jewel from its case. Not only did the colours of youth beam on her face, but health daily metamorphosed her limbs. The gentle flow of a generous life-fluid slowly puffed out her rosy and transparent skin, and all the springs of life, relaxed by three years' suffering, regained their elasticity with visible joy.

The witnesses of this miraculous transfiguration blessed science, but the happiest of all was probably

Dr. le Bris. The recovery of Germaine appeared to the others a hope, to him alone a certainty. He daily verified with a stethoscope the decrease of the malady ; he saw the cure in its causes and effects ; he measured as with a compass the ground he had regained from death.

On the 31st of August, the Doctor, happy as a conqueror, went down into the town ; for though he liked the country, he did not disdain a walk on the Esplanade to the sound of the military fifes and bagpipes On seeing the smoke of the steamers, he fancied he was drawing nearer to Paris. He willingly dined with the English officers, and with equal willingness lounged about the streets. He admired the soldiers all attired in white, with straw hats, yellow gloves, and varnished slippers, at the hour when these worthy fellows went to market with their little families. He refreshed his eye with the splendid display of green fruit, which the tradespeople keep in a state of truly English cleanliness ; one rubs the plums on his sleeve to make them glisten, while another dusts the rosy velvet of the peaches with a hat-brush. It is an admirable medley of melons large as pumpkins, lemons large as melons, plums large as lemons, and grapes large as plums. Perhaps, too, the young doctor regarded with some degree of satisfaction the pretty Greek girls leaning out of their windows from a framework of flowering cactus. In this primitive country, the maidens do not hesitate to throw kisses to a passing stranger, as the flower-girls of Florence fling bouquets into his carriage. If their father see them, he boxes their ears sharply in the name of morality, and that imparts a little variety to the scene.

While the Doctor was thus innocently amusing himself, Count Dandolo, Captain Brétignières, and the Vitrés were dining with the Villaneras. Gaston had no appetite, but Germaine enjoyed her dinner—he, poor fellow, dined with his eyes.

The conversation grew very interesting over the dessert. Count Dandolo described English policy in the East, and showed the Great Nation established at Hong Kong, Macao, Canton, and everywhere.

" You will see," he said, " or, at any rate, our children will see, the English masters of China and Japan."

" Stop there !" Captain Brétignières interrupted ; " what shall we give to France ?"

" All she will ask—that is to say, nothing. France is a disinterested country, passing her life in conquering the world, but scrupulously avoiding to keep anything for herself."

" Let us understand each other, Count. France has ever been free from egotism, she has done more for civilization than any other country in Europe, and has never asked for her reward. The Universe is our debtor, we have supplied it with ideas for the last three or four hundred years, and we have received nothing in exchange. When I think that we have not even the Ionian Islands !"

" You had them, Captain, and did not wish to keep them."

" Ah ! if I only had my two legs."

" What would you do, Captain ?" the Dowager asked,

" What would I do, Madame! My country has no ambition, so I would have it for her. I would give her the Ionian Isles, Malta, India, China, and Japan, and not suffer an universal monarchy."

" The Captain," Germaine said, "reminds me of that preceptor whose pupil had stolen a fig. He scolded him for his gluttony, and ate the fig as the peroration."

The Captain checked himself; he was red up to the ears : "I believe," he said, " that I went further than my thoughts. Where were we?"

" We were everywhere," Count Dandolo replied.

" Quite correct, as we were talking of England. Do you suppose that if the affair of Ky-Tcheou had happened to an English vessel, they would have been satisfied with bombarding the town? Not such fools! England would have gained from it a good commercial treaty, five millions in cash, and fifty leagues of territory."

" Do you think so?" M. Dandolo asked.

" I am certain."

" Well! what is the argument? We seem of the same opinion."

" What is the story about Ky-Tcheou?" Germaine asked.

" Have you not read it, Madame?"

" The only newspaper we read is yourself, Count."

" Well! Ky-Tcheou is a grand affair. The Chinese killed two French missionaries and a French officer; and the French razed the town—people are asking what will come of it all; and I think just nothing at all."

Count Villanera mixed in the conversation for the first time. "Is the affair you are talking about at all recent?" he asked Count Dandolo.

"Quite fresh; it arrived by the last mail. Have you heard nothing about the *Naiad* and the death of Captain Chermidy?"

The Count de Villanera turned pale. Germaine watched him closely to detect a symptom of joy; the old Countess rose from the table, and Count Dandolo went into the drawing-room, without telling the story of Ky-Tcheou.

Germaine took advantage of the moment when coffee was being served to her guests to take her husband off into the garden. The sun had set some two hours, and the night was warm as a summer day. They sat down on a rustic bench over-looking the sea; the moon had not yet appeared on the horizon, but shooting stars traversed the sky in every direction, and the sea illumined the beach with its phosphorescent glare.

Don Diego was still perfectly stunned by the news he had heard : he had received a violent shock, but the impression had been so sudden that he could not explain it to himself, and did not yet know whether it were pleasure or pain. He resembled a man who has fallen from a roof and feels himself all over to see if he be dead or alive. A thousand hurried reflections confusedly crossed his mind, like torches which pass through the night without dissipating the darkness. Germaine was not a whit calmer or more re-assured : she felt that the question of her living or dying would be decided within an hour, and that her physician was not M. le

Bris but the Count de Villanera. Still, these two young beings, shaken to the bottom of their hearts by a violent emotion, remained for some instants side by side in a profound silence. A fisherman, who was coasting the shore, must certainly have taken them for two happy lovers absorbed in the contemplation of th·ir bliss.

Germaine was the first to speak; she turned to her husband, took his hands in hers, and said in a choking voice—

"Don Diego, did you know it?"

He replied, "No, Germaine. Had I known it, I should have told you, for I have no secrets from you."

"And what do you say to the news—has it relieved you or oppressed you?"

"I know not how to answer, and you throw me into a state of cruel embarrassment. Grant me time to recover and reckon with myself. This event can cause me no pleasure, as you know; but if I were to say it oppressed me, you would conclude from it that I had formed engagements dependent on this fatal event—is not that your thought?"

"I am not quite sure what I think, Don Diego. My heart beats so fiercely, that it would be difficult for me to hear anything else. The only thing I see clearly, is that that woman is free. If she promised you to become a widow soon, she has kept her word before you. She is the first to arrive at the rendezvous you gave her, and I fear——"

"You fear?"

"I fear that I am in the way, as my living keeps

you from your happiness, and my health robs you even of hope."

"Your life and your health are presents from God, Germaine; a miracle of Heaven has saved you; and now that I know what a woman you are, I bless the decrees of Providence from the bottom of my heart."

"I thank you, Don Diego; I recognise you in this gentle and religious language. You are too good a Christian to revolt against a miracle. But do you regret nothing? Speak to me candidly, for I am well enough to hear everything."

"I only regret one thing—that I did not give you my first love."

"How truly kind you are! that woman was never worthy of you. Though I never saw her, I detest her instinctively and despise her."

"You must not despise her, Germaine. I no longer love her, because my heart is filled with you, and there is no room for the image of another woman; but I assure you, you do wrong to despise her."

"Why should I have more indulgence for her than the world has? She failed in all her duties and deceived the honest man who gave her his name. How can a woman betray her husband?"

"She is culpable in the sight of the world; but I dare not blame her, for she loved me."

"Ah! who would not love you, my friend? You are so good, so noble, so great, so handsome! Nay, do not shake your head; my taste is not worse than another woman's, and I know what I am saying. You are not like either Dr. le Bris, or Gaston de Vitré, or

Spiro Dandolo, or any of those men who meet with success among women, and yet it was on seeing you for the first time that I understood how man is the noblest work of creation."

"You like me, then, a little, Germaine?"

"A long time—since the first day you came to Sanglié House. And yet what you came to us for was very wrong. When the Doctor proposed the bargain to my parents, I fancied I was about to marry a wicked man. I promised to myself that I would endure you patiently and leave you without regret. But when I saw you in the salon, I felt ashamed for you, and regretted that so worthless a calculation had crossed a mind so noble and so intelligent. Then I made up my mind to treat you ill—do you know why? I should have died of vexation if you had guessed I loved you. That was not in our bargain. During the whole of our tour in Italy, I strove to cause you pain, and can you believe I should have behaved with so much ingratitude if you had been indifferent to me? But I was furious at seeing that you merely treated me so kindly as a salve to your conscience, and then, in spite of myself, I thought of the other who was awaiting you at Paris. And then, too, I was afraid of growing into a pleasant state of love and happiness which death might come to interrupt. Besides, I was very ill and suffered cruelly!

"The day when you wept out of the carriage window, I saw it, and felt inclined to ask your pardon, and leap on your neck, but my pride restrained me. I am the first of my blood, recollect, who was ever sold for money. Yes, I nearly betrayed myself that evening at Pompeii—do you remember it? I have forgotten nothing, neither your kind words nor my harshness; your tender and patient care, nor the cruel way in which I treated you. I offered you a very bitter cup, and you have drunk it to the dregs. I will allow that I have not been very happy either; I was not sure of you—feared I might be mistaken as to the sense of your kindness, and take marks of pity for testimony of love. What reassured me slightly was the pleasure you found in remaining near me. When you walked in the garden round my chair, I followed you with the corner of my eye, and frequently feigned sleep to draw you closer. I needed not to open my eyes to know you were near me, for I could see you through my eyelids. When you are near me, my heart dilates and swells till it fills my whole bosom; when you speak, your voice tingles in my ears, and I feel intoxicated by listening to you. Whenever my hand touches yours, I feel a throb through my whole body, and a gentle quivering at the roots of my hair. When you retire for a moment, and I can neither see nor hear you, there is a great vacuum around me, and I feel a want which overwhelms me. And now, Don Diego, tell me if I love you, for you have more experience than I, and cannot make a mistake in such a matter. I am only a little ignorant girl; but you must remember whether this were the way in which you were loved at Paris."

This simple confession fell on Don Diego's heart like a dew; he was so deliciously refreshed by it that he not only forgot his present cares, but also his past pleasures. A new light shone in upon his mind: he compared at a glance his old amours, agitated and turbid like a storm-swelled stream, to the gentle limpidness of legitimate happiness. It is the history of all young husbands: the day on which a man rests his head on the conjugal pillow, he perceives with agreeable surprise that he never slept well before.

The Count tenderly kissed Germaine's hand, and said :—

"Yes, you love me; and no one ever loved me as you do. You bear me into a new world, full of honourable delights and remorseless pleasures. I know not if I have saved your life ; but you have amply paid your debt by opening my blind eyes to the holy light of love. Let us love, Germaine, and give free rein to our hearts. Let us forget the whole world to belong to each other. Let us close our ears to all the rumours of the world, whether they come from China or Paris. This is our earthly Paradise, so let us live in it for ourselves, and bless the Hand that placed us in it."

"Yes, let us live for ourselves," she said, "and for those who love us. I should not be so happy if I had not our mother and our child with us? Ah, I loved them openly from the first day. How like you they are ! When little Gomez comes to play in the garden, I fancy I see your smile moving in the grass. I am very happy that I adopted him. That woman will never take him from me ? The law has given him to me for ever ; he is my heir, my only son !"

"No, Germaine," he replied ; "he is your eldest son !"

Germaine stretched out her arms to her husband,

clung round his neck, drew him to her, and gently pressed her lips upon his forehead. But the emotion of this first kiss was stronger than the poor convalescent : her eyes grew dim, and her whole body gave way. When she had recovered from this shock, she returned to the house on her husband's arm ; she hung upon it with her whole weight, like a child learning to walk.

" You see," she said, " I am still very weak, in spite of appearances. I fancied myself strong, and yet, you see, a mere nothing of happiness overpowers me. Do not speak to me too kindly and render me too happy : wait for that till I am perfectly restored. It would be too dreadful to die just when life is beginning so well. Now I will hurry on my recovery, and take the greatest possible care of myself. Do you go back to the drawing-room ; I am going to my bed-room. To-morrow we shall meet again."

She went to her room, and threw herself on the bed, all panting and all confused. A luminous spot glistening in a corner attracted her attention ; the flame of the lamp was reflected from the small globe of the iodometer. She blessed this beneficent apparatus, which had restored her to life, and would give her back her strength in a few days. Suddenly the idea struck her that she would hasten her recovery by taking a large dose of iodine without the doctor's knowledge. She arranged the apparatus, drew it to her bed, and eagerly drank-in the violet vapour. She inhaled it with delight ; she felt neither disgust nor fatigue ; she swallowed long draughts of health and vigour. She

was delighted to prove to the doctor that he had been
too prudent. She committed an act of heroic madness,
and risked her life through love for Don Diego.

No one ever knew what quantity of iodine she
inhaled, or how long she prolonged this fatal impru-
dence. When the old Countess slipped out of the
drawing-room to look after her, she found the apparatus
broken on the ground, and the invalid a prey to a
violent fever. They did what they could for her till
the Doctor came back about midnight; and all the
guests slept at the Villa to hear how she went on.
The Doctor was terrified by Germaine's agitation, and
did not know whether to attribute it to the immoderate
use of iodine, or to some dangerous emotion. Madame
de Villanera secretly accused Count Dandolo; Don
Diego accused himself.

The next day Dr. le Bris recognised an inflammation
in the lungs, which might cause death; he called in
Dr. Delviniotis and two of his colleagues. The physicians differed as to the cause of her illness; but not
one ventured to predict her recovery. M. le Bris had
lost his head, like the captain of a vessel who finds
breakers at the very entrance of the harbour. Dr.
Delviniotis, a little calmer, though he could not refrain
from weeping, timidly held out a gleam of hope :—

"Perhaps," he said, "we have to deal with an
adhesive inflammation which will re-form the cavities
and repair all the disorders caused by the illness."

The poor little Doctor shook his head mournfully as
he listened to this opinion : it would be just as much
use saying to an architect : "Your house is out of the

perpendicular ; but an earthquake may happen which will set it to rights." Everybody agreed that the invalid was entering on a crisis ; but not even Dr. Delviniotis ventured to affirm that it would not terminate fatally.

Germaine was in a state of delirium, and recognised nobody. In all the men who approached her she fancied she saw Don Diego ; in all the women, Madame Chermidy. Her distraught sentences were a singular mixture of tenderness and menaces. She asked every moment for her son; but when the little Marquis was brought to her, she angrily repulsed him.

" That is not he," she said ; " bring me my eldest son ; the woman's son. I am sure she has taken him back."

The child vaguely comprehended his little mother's danger, though he had no notion of death ; but as he saw everybody weeping, he cried his little heart out almost.

At that time could be seen how dear the young wife was to all who surrounded her. For eight days the friends of the family encamped around her, sleeping where they could, eating what came to hand, occupied solely with the patient, and not at all with themselves. Captain Brétignières could not keep quiet for an instant ; he stumped about the house and the garden, and the sound of his wooden leg was incessantly heard. Mr. Stevens gave up his business, his pleasures, and his habits. Madame de Vitré became nurse under the orders of the Countess. The two Dandolos ran to the town morning and night to seek physicians who could offer no advice, and remedies which could not be used. The people in the neighbourhood were in the deepest anxiety ; news of Germaine's state was carried to all the surrounding houses every morning and night. From all sides flocked in family remedies, and those secret panaceas handed down from father to son.

Don Diego and Gaston de Vitré bore a singular resemblance to each other in their grief ; you might have taken them for the two brothers of the dying girl. Both lived apart, seated beneath a tree, or on the sand, plunged into a dry and tearless stupor. If the Count had had leisure to be jealous, he would have been so of the despair of this boy ; but everybody was too much occupied with Germaine's danger to watch his neighbour's face. Madame de Vitré alone, now and then, directed an anxious glance upon her son, and then ran back again to Germaine's bed, as if a secret instinct told her that she would in this way benefit Gaston most.

The Dowager Countess was a terrible object. This tall black woman, dirty and unkempt, allowed her hair to hang in masses from under her cap. She wept no more than her son, but a poem of grief could be read in her haggard eyes. She spoke to no one, she saw no one, she allowed the guests to attend to themselves. Her whole thoughts were concentrated on Germaine ; her whole soul struggled against the present danger with a will of iron. Never did the Genius of Good borrow a face more stern and terrible, and on it might be traced a furious devotion, an exasperated tenderness. She was no longer a woman or a nurse, but a female demon wrestling with death.

Mathieu Mantoux's face, however, gently expanded in the sun ; and all his masters having taken on themselves the duties of servants, this faithful domestic indulged in the leisure of a master. He inquired every morning as to Germaine's health, solely to know if he would not soon come into his pension. He attributed his mistress's death to the glass of sugared water he had prepared so patiently for her every evening, and thought, as he rubbed his hands, that every man who knew how to wait gains his point. At midday he took his second breakfast, and to digest it at his ease, he walked for an hour or two round the little farm on which he had fixed his desires. He noticed that the fences were in very bad order, and promised he would put them in thorough repair in order to keep thieves out.

On the 6th September, Dr. Delviniotis himself lost all hope. Mantoux was aware of it, and wrote a note to a certain stout lady in Paris, while on the same day Dr. le Bris wrote to the Duke de la Tour :—

MY LORD,—I dare not call you to me. By the time you receive this all will be over, Break the news to the Duchess."

CHAPTER XI.

THE WIDOW CHERMIDY.

Mantoux's letter and the formal promise of Germaine's death arrived at Madame Chermidy's on September 12.

The fair Honorine had lost all hope and patience; she received no letters from Corfu; she was without news of her lover and her son; and the doctor, occupied with more important cares, had not even written to congratulate her on her widowhood. She began to suspect M. de Villanera; she compared herself to Calypso, Medea, and the fair Ariadne; indeed, to all the deserted beauties of mythology. She felt amazed sometimes at finding that her spite was turning into love, and surprised herself at times sighing though no one was present, and in all good faith. The remembrance of the three years she had passed with the Count strangely tickled the memory of her heart. Among other acts of folly she regretted having curbed him in too tight, and hung the prize too high, not having given him happiness to repletion, and killed him with tenderness. "It is my fault," she said; "I accustomed him to do without me. If I had minded, I should have become the necessity of his life. I should have merely wanted to give the signal, and he would quit mother, wife, everything."

She asked herself frequently whether absence did
not injure her in Don Diego's favour, and studied the
vulgar proverb, "Out of sight, out of mind." She
thought of embarking for the Ionian Islands, falling
like a bombshell on her lover's house, and carrying him
off by sheer strength. A quarter of an hour would
be sufficient to rekindle the badly-extinguished fires,
and renew an association which was as yet only interrupted. She fancied herself engaged with Germaine
and the old Countess ; she overwhelmed them by her
eloquence, beauty, and strength of will. She took her
son in her arms, fled with him, and the child's irresistible smile carried off the father. "Who knows,"
she said, "whether a well-acted scene might not kill
the invalid ? Women in good health will faint at the
theatre, so a well-acted drama of my invention might
send her into an eternal fainting fit."

A feeling which was more human, and yet less probable, caused her to regret the absence of her son.
She had given birth to him ; she was his mother after
all, and regretted that she had surrendered him for the
benefit of another woman. Maternal love finds a
lodging everywhere ; it is a guest without any fas-
tidiousness, and allows the vicinity of the worst
passions : it lives quite at its ease in the most depraved
heart and most ruined soul. Madame Chermidy wept
a few tears of good alloy on thinking that she had
alienated the fortunes of her son and abdicated the
name of mother.

She was seriously unhappy—it is only on the stage
that real unhappiness is the sole privilege of virtue.

She had no want of distractions and had only to choose, but she knew by experience that pleasure affords no consolation. For more than ten years her life had been noisy and excited as a *fête*; but her peace of mind had paid all the expenses. There is nothing so empty, restless, and miserable as the existence of a woman who makes pleasure the one object of life. The ambition which had supported her since her marriage, henceforth was but a slight resource to her; it was a broken reed, as she found too late. She was rich enough to disdain any increase of fortune; there is, after all, but slight difference between twenty thousand and ten thousand a year; a few more horses in the stable, a few more servants in the hall, add scarcely anything to the happiness of the master. A good name to show off in the world would have amused her for some time, and she thought more than once of procuring one legitimately, and she had fifty to choose from, for there are always names for sale in Paris. But she had a right to be difficult in her selection, for had she not been almost Countess de Villanera? She could not make up her mind.

In the meanwhile she had a fancy to give a public successor to Don Diego, for perhaps he would come to reclaim his property, when he found another man enjoying the usufruct. But she feared she would thus be supplying the enemy with arms. Germaine was not yet cured, and she must not close the door of marriage. Besides, though she sought carefully around her, she did not find a single man worthy a caprice or fit to succeed M. de Villanera, even for a day. The supernumeraries who visited her salon never knew how near they had been to happiness.

Hence, she found nothing better to occupy her leisure time than to complete the moral ruin of the old Duke. She accomplished the task she had laid down for herself with the minute attention, patient care, and indefatigable perseverance of that idle sultana who in her master's absence, plucked out, one by one, the feathers of an old paroquet.

She would certainly have preferred avenging herself directly on Germaine; but Germaine was far away. If the Duchess had been within her reach, she would have bestowed her preference on the Duchess. But the Duchess never left her house except to go to church, and Madame Chermidy could not meet her there. She might starve the Ducal household, but the operation would require time; for, in finding money again, the La Tours had regained their credit. The fair enemy of the family had only the Duke in her power. She swore to make him lose his head, and succeeded.

In the Russian baths, when the patient quits the red-hot bath-room, after his body has been gradually accustomed to a high temperature, when the heat has dilated all the pores of the skin, and the blood courses furiously through his veins—he is quietly placed beneath a *douche* of cold water; it falls on his head and chills him to the very marrow. Madame Chermidy treated the duke by the same method; and though we are told it succeeds with the Russians, the poor old man was not improved by it. He was the

victim of the most odious coquetry that ever tortured
the heart of man. Madame Chermidy persuaded him
that she loved him. Lump affirmed it on oath, and,
had he consented to take words as payment, he would
have been the happiest sexagenarian in Paris. He
passed his life at Madame Chermidy's, and suffered
martyrdom; he daily expended there as much eloquence
and passion, reasoning and entreaty, true and false
logic, as there are in the whole of the "New Heloïse,"
and every evening he was dismissed with fair words.
He swore he would never return; he spent a long
sleepless night in cursing the cause of his suffering, and
the next day he ran to his executioner with senile
impotence. All his intellect, will, and vices were absorbed and confounded in this exclusive passion; he
was no longer husband, father, man, or gentleman—
he was simply the *patito* of Madame Chermidy.

After a summer of daily suffering, his intellectual
faculties had sensibly given way. He had nearly
entirely lost his memory; at least, he forgot everything
which did not bear reference to his love. He took no
interest in what went on around him; private and
public affairs, his house, his wife, his daughter, all were
indifferent and strange to him. The Duchess nursed
him like a child, when he by chance remained with
her; but, unfortunately, he was not yet childish enough
to be locked up.

When he received Dr. le Bris' letter, he read it
twice or thrice without understanding it, and, had the
Duchess been near him, he would have begged her to
read and to explain it to him. But he broke the seal

at his own door, as he was hastening to Madame Chermidy's, and was in too great haste to turn back. By repeatedly perusing it, he guessed that it referred to his daughter, but he only shrugged his shoulders and said, as he hurried on, "that Le Bris is always the same. I do not know what cause of dislike he has against my daughter. The proof that she will not die is, that she is quite well." Still he reflected that the doctor might speak the truth, and this idea terrified him. "It is a great misfortune for us," he said, as he hurried on still faster. "I am an inconsolable father. There is no time to lose. I will go and tell it to Honorine ; she will pity me, for she has a good heart. She will wipe away my tears, and, who knows—— ?" He smiled stupidly to himself as he entered the drawing-room.

Never had Madame Chermidy been so radiant or so lovely. Her face was a sun ; triumph sparkled in her eyes ; her chair seemed like a throne, and her voice resounded like a clarion. She rose as the Duke entered ; her feet hardly touched the ground, and her head, superb in its joy, seemed to rise to the chandelier. The old man stopped, panting and paralysed, on seeing her thus transfigured. He muttered a few unintelligible words, and fell heavily into an easy chair.

Madame Chermidy seated herself by his side.

"Good day, your Grace !" she said to him ; "good day, and good-bye !"

He turned pale, and repeated stupidly, "Good-bye ?"

"Yes, good-bye. You do not ask me where I am going."

" Yes !"

" Well ! I will satisfy you ; I am going to Corfu."

" By the way," he said, "I believe my daughter is
dead ; the doctor wrote to me so this morning.   I am
very miserable, Honorine, and you must take pity on
me."

" Oh yes ; you are unhappy ! and the Duchess, too,
is unhappy ! and the old Villanera will weep black
tears down her swarthy cheek.   But I laugh, I triumph,
I bury, I marry, I reign !   She is dead ! she has paid
her debt at last ! she restores me all she took from me !
I return into possession of my lover and my son !
Why do you look at me with such astonished eyes ?
Do you fancy I shall put any constraint on myself ?   It
is quite enough to have swallowed my rage for eight
months.   All the worse for those whom my happiness
offends : they need only shut their eyes ; I am bursting !"

This impudent joy restored to the old man a gleam
of reason.   He rose firmly on his feet, and said to the
widow :

" Do you really know what you are doing ?   You
are rejoicing in my presence at the death of my
daughter !"

" And you," she replied, impudently, " used to
rejoice in her life.   Who was it that so carefully
brought me tidings of her ?   Who was it that came
to tell me, ' She is better ?'   Who compelled me to
read her letters and Dr. le Bris's ?   For eight months
you have been assassinating me with her health, and
the least you can do is to grant me a quarter of an
hour to rejoice over her death."

" Honorine, you are a horrible woman !"

" I am as I am. If your daughter had lived, as I was threatened with, she would not have been hidden from me. She would have driven out every day in the park with Don Diego and my son, and I should have seen that from my carriage. She would have put on her visiting cards the name of Villanera, which is mine, for I gained it fairly. And yet you would prevent me taking my revenge !"

" Then you still love the Count ?"

" Poor Duke! do you fancy a man like Don Diego can be forgotten between to-day and to-morrow ? Do you think a woman brings into the world a child like mine to make it a present to a sickly girl ? Do you suppose that I prayed for the death of my husband during three years—I who never pray—not to enjoy my liberty ? Do you imagine that Chermidy went to be killed by the Chinese that I might remain a widow for ever ?"

" You are going to marry Count Villanera ?"

" I flatter myself so."

" Then, what will become of me ?"

" You, my good fellow ? go and console your wife ; you ought to have begun with that."

" What am I to say to her, Honorine ?"

" Whatever you please. Good-bye, I have my boxes to pack. Do you want any money ?"

The Duke displayed his disgust by shrugging his shoulders. Madame Chermidy noticed it.

" Our money is repugnant to you, I suppose ?" she said. " As you please ! you shall have no more."

The old man went off, he knew not whither, just like a drunkard, and wandered about the streets of Paris till night. About ten o'clock he began to feel hungry, so he hired a cab, and went to the club. He was so changed that Baron de Sanglié alone recognised him.

"What on earth is the matter with you?" he asked the Duke. "Why, you cannot stand firm. Sit down here, and let us talk."

"Very willingly," the Duke said.

"How is the Duchess? I have only just come from the country, and have not paid a single visit yet."

"How the Duchess is?"

"Yes, how is she?"

"She is going to cry."

"Oh! he is mad!" the Baron thought.

The Duke added, without changing his tone, "I believe that Germaine is dead, and Honorine is glad of it. I consider that shocking, and I told her so myself."

"Germaine! Come, my poor friend, think of what you say. Germaine—the Countess de Villancra—dead!"

"Honorine is the Countess de Villanera: she is going to marry the Count. Stay, I have the letter in my pocket; but what do you think of Honorine's conduct?"

The Baron read the doctor's letter at a glance: "How long have you learned this?" he asked the Duke.

"This morning, on going to Honorine's."

" And does the Duchess know anything of it

" No! I do not know how to tell it her. I was going to ask Honorine——"

" Oh! deuce take Honorine !"

" That's what I say."

The Baron was called to cut in at whist, but he replied that he was busy, and asked some one to take his place. He wished to finish the conference ; but the Duke interrupted by saying, in a hollow voice, " I am hungry, I have not eaten to-day."

" Are you sure ?"

" Yes ; order me some dinner ; and you must lend me some money, too, for I have none left."

" How !"

" Oh, I know ; I had a large fortune, but I have given it to Honorine."

The Duke devoured with the voracious appetite of a madman, and after dinner his ideas grew cleare   His mind was more worn than ill.   He told the B ron or the insensate passion that had possessed him for the last six months, and explained to him how he had stripped himself of everything on behalf of Madame Chermidy.

The Baron, who was a worthy man, was much shocked at hearing that the family which he had seen raised again a few months back, had fallen lower than ever.   Above all, he pitied the Duchess, who must inevitably succumb beneath so many blows.   He took on himself to break to her gradually the illness and death of Germaine, and applied himself to restore the Duke's weakened intellect.   He reassured him as to the consequences of his mad generosity ; it was evident that

the Count would not leave his father-in-law in want.
At the same time he studied, from the Duke's con-
fessions and reticences, the singular character of Madame
Chermidy.

The authority of a healthy mind is omnipotent over
a weak brain, and thus, after two hours' conversation,
the Duke unravelled the chaos of his ideas, lamented
the death of his daughter, feared for the health of his
wife, regretted the follies he had committed, and
esteemed the widow Chermidy at her true value. The
Baron took him to his door, well doctored, if not
thoroughly cured.

At an early hour the next morning the Baron paid
the Duchess a visit. He stopped the old Duke on the
threshold as he was going out, and compelled him to
turn back with him. He did not leave him out of
sight for three days; he took him about, amused him,
and succeeded in diverting him from the sole thought
that agitated him. He took him eventually to the
house of the pitiless Honorine, and proved to him by a
conversation with the porter that she had set out with
Lump for the Ionian Islands.

The Duke was less affected by this intelligence than
might have been expected ; he lived quietly at home,
paid great attention to his wife, and proved to her with
extreme delicacy that Germaine was not yet thoroughly
cured, and evil news might yet arrive. He took an
interest in the minutest details of the household,
granted the necessity of making certain purchases,
borrowed a hundred pounds from his friend Sanglié,
and started for Corfu on the morning of the 20th
September, without saying a word to anybody.

CHAPTER XII.

THE LADIES' BATTLE.

ON the 8th September, Germaine, who was condemned without appeal, deluded the fears of her physicians and her friends—she began to grow better. The fever that had devoured her subsided in a few hours, like those great tropical storms which uproot trees, overthrow houses, and shake mountains to their foundations, but which a sunbeam arrests in the fury of their progress.

This happy revolution was effected so suddenly that Don Diego and the Countess Dowager could not believe in it. Though man accustoms himself more quickly to happiness than to suffering, their hearts remained for some days in a state of suspense. They feared to be the dupes of a false joy; they dared not congratulate themselves on a miracle so little expected, and they asked each other whether this apparent recovery were not the supreme effort of a being clutching at life—the last flare of an expiring lamp.

But Dr. le Bris and M. Delviniotis recognised by sure signs that the sufferings of this poor little body were really ended. The inflammation had repaired in a week all the ravages of a long illness—the crisis had saved Germaine—the earthquake had restored the building to the perpendicular.

The girl found it quite natural to live and be cured. Thanks to the delirium of fever, she had gone through the valley of the shadow without perceiving it, and the violence of the illness had removed the feeling of danger. She woke up like a child on the brink of a well, without measuring the depth of the abyss. When told that she had been all but dead, and that her friends had despaired of her, she was much astonished; but when promised a long life and no more suffering, she tenderly gazed on a crucifix hanging near a bed, and said, with gentle and confiding gaiety,—" I deserve it, for I have passed through my purgatory."

She regained her strength in a short time, and health soon tinged her cheeks again. It seemed as if nature were hastening to bedeck her for happiness. She entered once more on possession of life with the impetuous joy of a claimant who leaps at one bound on the throne of his fathers. She would have liked to be everywhere at once, to enjoy all the pleasures offered her, movement and repose, solitude and society, the dazzling brightness of day and the serene lustre of night. Her little hands clung joyously to everything that surrounded her; she lavished her endearments on her husband, her mother-in-law, her child, and her friends. At times she wept without any motive, but they were sweet tears; little Gomez kissed them away from the corners of her eyes, as a bird drinks the dew in the cup of a flower.

Everything affords pleasure to the convalescent; the most indifferent functions of life are a source of ineffable delight to a man who has all but died. All the senses vibrate deliciously on the least contact with the external world. The heat of the sun appears to him more pleasant than a cloak of ermine ; the light rejoices his sight like a caress ; the perfumes of the flowers intoxicate him ; the sounds of nature reach his ear like a pleasant melody ; and bread seems to him a dainty regale.

Those who had shared Germaine's sufferings felt themselves regenerated with her, and her convalescence soon restored the health of all the sharers in her agony. She saw none but cloudless brows around her, and joy caused all hearts to beat in unison. All the fatigue and pain so lately endured were forgotten ; gaiety was mistress of the house. The first fine day removed from every face any trace of anxiety and tears. The guests did not think about returning to their houses, for they believed they belonged to the family. United by happiness as they had been by uneasiness, they surrounded Germaine like a happy family, an adored child. On the day that a letter was written to the Duchess, to announce the recovery of her daughter, each wished to add a word for the happy mother, and the pen passed from hand to hand. This letter reached Paris on September 22nd, two days after the old Duke's eclipse.

Madame Chermidy and her inseparable Lump landed at Corfu on the evening of the 24th. The widow had packed up in all haste, and had scarce spared the time to get in 5000l. to pay Mantoux and any unforeseen expenses. Lump advised her to await more positive intelligence at Paris ; but people believe so gladly what they desire, that Madame Chermidy regarded Germaine as buried. From Trieste to Corfu she lived on deck, glass in hand, for she wished to be the first to sight land. She was inclined to stop all the vessels that passed to asked them if they had no letters addressed to her. She inquired whether they would arrive in the morning, for she did not fancy she could endure waiting a night, and intended to drive straight to the Villa Dandolo. Her impatience was so evident that the cabin passengers christened her the "heiress," and it was whispered that she was proceeding to Corfu to take possession of a large fortune.

The sea was very rough for a couple of days, and everybody was ill except Germaine's heiress, for she had not time to feel the rolling. Perhaps her feet did not even feel the deck, for she was so light that she hovered instead of walking. When she fell asleep by any accident, she dreamt that she was floating in the air.

The boat cast anchor at nightfall, and it was past nine o'clock before the passengers and their baggage were landed. The sight of the scattered lights burning about the town produced a disagreeable effect on Madame Chermidy; for when we reach the end of a journey, hope, which had till then buoyed us up, fails us of a sudden, and we fall suddenly on the reality. What seemed to us most certain now appears dubious; we no longer calculate on anything, and begin to feel prepared for everything. A chill falls upon us, whatever may be the ardour of the passions that animate us; we are tempted to put everything in the worst light; we regret we have come, and would like to turn back. This impression is the more painful if the country we are going to is quite strange to us; when no one is awaiting us at the landing-place, and we are left a prey to those polyglottic porters who buzz around passengers. Our first feeling is a blending of vexation, disgust, and discouragement. Madame Chermidy reached the Trafalgar Hotel in a very uncomfortable state.

She hoped to hear there of Germaine's death ; but she learned before all that the French language is not very widely spread in the hotels of Corfu. Madame Chermidy and Lump, between them, only knew one foreign language, Provencal, which was not of much service to them in this country. Hence they were compelled to send for an interpreter, and sup in the meanwhile. The interpreter arrived when the landlord had gone to bed ; he got up growling, and found it hard to be awoke for business that did not concern him. He knew neither the Count nor the Countess de Villanera ; and they could not have come to the island, for all travellers of distinction lodged at the Trafalgar Hotel. It was not possible that the Count and Countess, if persons of quality, could have stayed elsewhere. The English, the Albion, the Victoria, were establishments of the lowest order, unworthy to receive the Count and Countess de Villanera.

The landlord went back to bed, and the interpreter offered to run and obtain some information. He remained away the best part of the night, and Lump went to sleep while waiting for him. Madame Chermidy gnawed at the bit, and was amazed that a person with £5000 in her pocket-book could not obtain a simple piece of information. She roused poor Lump,

who was entirely worn out. Lump advised her to go
to bed, instead of tormenting herself.

" You may be quite sure," she said, " that if the little
one has removed to another world, the whole town has
not gone into mourning for her. We shall only hear
about her in the country. Everybody must know the
Villa Dandolo ; so go to bed quietly ; it will be day
to-morrow. What risk do you run ? If she is dead, I
am quite sure she will not come to life again in the
night."

Madame Chermidy was about to follow her cousin's
advice, when the *valet de place* came with much importance to tell her that the Count and Countess de Villanera had landed in the island in the month of April
last, with their physician and entire household ; they
were very ill ; they had been taken to the Villa Dandolo, and they must all be dead a long time ago, unless
they were better. The impatient widow turned the
lacquey out, threw herself on her bed, and slept but badly.

The next day she hired a carriage, and drove out to
the Villa Dandolo. The coachman was unable to tell
her what interested her most ; and the peasants she met
listened to her questions without understanding them.
She took every house she saw for the Villa Dandolo,
for all the houses are like each other on this island.
When her driver pointed out to her a slate roof em-
bowered in trees, she pressed her heart with both hands.
She attentively consulted the physiognomy of the land-
scape to read the great news she burned to hear ; but,
unfortunately, gardens, woods, and high roads are im-
passive witnesses of our joy and grief. If they pay any

interest to our fate, they hide the fact very closely from us, for the trees in a park do not assume mourning on the death of their master.

Madame Chermidy was angry at the slowness of the horses, and would have liked to gallop up the zigzag leading to the villa. She could hardly remain in the carriage ; she flew from one window to the other, interrogating the houses and the fields, and seeking a human face. At length she jumped to the ground, ran to the villa, found every door open, and did not meet a soul. She returned and traversed the north garden— it was deserted. A little doorway and a flight of steps led to the southern garden. She rushed down them and wandered through the grounds.

She perceived beneath the shade of an old orange tree near the sea-shore, a lady dressed in white, walking backwards and forwards, with a book in her hand. She was too far off to recognise the face, but the colour of the dress caused her anxious thought— people do not wear white in a house of mourning. All the observations she had made during the last few minutes contradicted each other ; the almost utter abandonment of the villa seemed to evidence Germaine's death. The doors were open, the domestics absent, the family gone away—where to ? Perhaps to Paris ! But how was it that nothing was known about it in the town ? Could Germaine have recovered ? Impossible, in so short a time. Was she still ill ? But in that case she would be nursed, and the doors not left open. She hesitated to advance to the white lady, when a child crossed the walk and rushed under the

trees like a startled rabbit crossing a woodland glade.
She recognised her son, and regained her boldness.
"What have I to fear, after all?" she thought; "no
one has the right to turn me out here. Whether she
is alive or dead, I am a mother, and have come to see
my son."

She walked straight up to the child. Little Gomez
was frightened on seeing this lady in black, and ran
crying to his mamma. Madame Chermidy went after
him and stopped short in the presence of Germaine.

Germaine was alone in the garden with the Marquis.
All the visitors had taken leave of her: the Countess
and her son were escorting Madame de Vitré home;
the doctor had gone into town with the Dandolos and
Dr. Delviniotis. The house was left to the servants,
and they were indulging in their siesta, according to
their habit, wherever the sun had surprised them.

Madame Chermidy recognised at the first glance the
girl she had only seen once, and whom she never
expected to see again in this world. Though she was
so resolute, and nature had endowed her with such a
vigorous mind, she fell back a good pace, like a soldier
in whose face the bridge he is just going to cross is
exploded. She was not the woman to nurse herself
with chimeras: she judged her position, and leaped at
one bound to the last consequences. She saw her rival
thoroughly cured, her lover confiscated, her son in the
hands of another woman, and her own fortune ruined.
The fall was the more rude because the ambitious fair
one fell from such a height. After piling mountains
on mountains up to the gates of heaven, the Titans in

the fall did not feel the less severely the lovin brand that routed them.

The hatred she nourished towards the young Countess since the day she had begun to fear her, suddenly assumed colossal proportions, like those theatrical trees which the machinist produces from the stage and forces up to the drops. The first idea that crossed her mind was that of a crime. She felt a strength centupled by rage quivering in her muscles. She asked herself why she did not tear down this fragile obstacle that separated her from happiness. For a second she became the sister of those Thyades who tore in fragments living tigers and lions. She repented she had left behind, at the Trafalgar Hotel, a Corsican poniard, a terrible plaything, which she displayed everywhere on her mantelpiece. The blade was blue like a watch-spring, long and pliant like the busk of a pair of stays; the hilt was of ebony incrusted with silver, and the sheath of oxidized platina. She ran in thought to this familiar weapon; she mentally seized it, and caressed it in imagination. Then she thought of the sea that so gently bathed the edge of the garden; nothing was more easy and tempting than to carry off Germaine, as an eagle bears a lamb to its nest, lay her in three feet of water, stifle her cries beneath the waves, and compress her struggles till a final convulsion made another Countess de Villanera.

Fortunately, the distance is further between thought and action than from the arm to the head. Besides, little Gomez was there, and his presence probably saved Germaine's life. More than once the limpid glance of a child has sufficed to paralyse a criminal hand. The most profligate beings have an involuntary respect for this sacred age, which is even more august than old age. The latter is like calm water which has allowed all the impurities of life to sink to the bottom; but infancy is a stream that has burst from the mountain side; which may be agitated without troubling it, because it is thoroughly pure. Old men have a knowledge of good and evil; while the ignorance of childhood is like the spotless snow of the Jungfrau, which no footprint has polluted, not even the claw-mark of a bird.

Madame Chermidy conceived, caressed, debated, and rejected the idea of a crime, while closing her parasol and bowing to Germaine, who did not know her.

Germaine received her with that expansive grace and openness of heart, which only the happy ones in this world can have. The visit of an unknown lady was not calculated to embarrass her, for she daily received kind neighbours, who had felt an interest in her recovery, and came to rejoice with her at her health. The widow stammered confusedly, owing to the tumult of her thoughts.

"Madame," she said, "you could not expect—I did not expect, myself—had I but known—Madame, I have just arrived from Paris—the Duke de la Tour, who honours me with his friendship——"

"You know my father, Madame," Germaine quickly interrupted her; "have you seen him recently?"

"Within a week."

"My poor father—how is he? He writes to us very rarely. Tell me about my mother!"

Madame Chermidy bit her lip.

" I did not expect," she went on, without replying, "to find you in such good health. The last letter the Duke received from Corfu—"

" Yes ; I was in a very low state, but I was refused admission to paradise. Pray sit down by my side— at the present moment my father and mother no longer feel alarm. Oh, I am really saved—but you can see it, I am sure. Look at me carefully."

" Yes, madame. After what we heard at Paris it is a miracle."

" A miracle of friendship and love. The Countess, my mother, is so kind ; my husband is so good to me."

" Ah ! that is a pretty boy playing there. Is he yours, madame ?"

Germaine rose from her seat, looked at the widow, and recoiled in horror, as if she had stepped on a viper.

" Madame," she said to the unknown, " you are Madame Chermidy !"

The widow rose in her turn, and marched straight on Germaine, as if to trample her under-foot. " Yes," she said, " I am the mother of the Marquis, and the wife, before heaven, of Don Diego. How did you recognise me ?"

" By the tone in which you spoke of your child."

This was said with so much gentleness that Madame Chermidy was affected with a strange feeling. Anger, surprise, and all the emotions that choked her, burst forth in one intense sob, and two large tears coursed down her cheeks. Germaine was not aware that people can cry from rage. She pitied her enemy, and said to her simply, " Poor creature."

The tears dried instantaneously, like drops of rain falling into a crater.

" Poor creature ! This to me !" Madame Chermidy replied, acridly. " Well, yes, I am to be pitied, because I have been deceived ; because my good faith has been abused ; because heaven and earth have conspired together to betray me ; because I have been robbed of name, fortune, the man I love, and the child I bore in grief and lamentation !"

Germaine was terrified at this explosion of wrath, and she turned her eyes toward the house, as if seeking aid.

" Madame," she said, trembling, " if you have come to my house for this purpose—"

" *Your* house ; perhaps you will call your servants to drive me from *your* house. In truth, that is admirable ! Why, it is *my* house ; you have nothing you do not derive from me ! Your husband, your child, your fortune, the very air you breathe, all come from me ; they are a pledge I intrusted to you ; you owe me everything and will never repay me ! You were vegetating in Paris on a wretched pallet ; the physicians condemned you to death, you had not three months to live. I was promised it ! Your father and mother would have died of hunger had it not been for me ! The La Tour family would now be but a pile of dust in the common ditch. I have given you everything : father, mother, husband, child, and life ; and you dare to tell me to my face that I am in *your* house. You must really be very ungrateful !"

It was difficult to reply to this savage eloquence.

Germaine crossed her arms on her chest, and said, "When I examine my conscience I cannot find myself guilty of anything save of recovering. I never contracted any engagements with you, as I meet you to-day for the first time. It is true that without you I should have been dead long ago ; but if you have saved me it was against your will, and the proof of it is that you have now come to reproach me with the air I breathe. Did you select me as wife for the Count de Villanera ? Perhaps you did ; but you chose me because you believed me hopelessly condemned. I do not owe you any gratitude for that. And now what can I do to be of service to you ? You can command me in everything, except dying."

"I ask nothing, I want nothing, I expect nothing."

"Then what did you come here to do ? Oh, I see! you expected to find me dead."

"I had a right to do so, but I ought to have made some inquiries about your family : the La Tours never paid their debts."

At this coarse remark Germaine lost patience.

"Madame," she said, "you see that I am quite well ; as you only came here to bury me, your journey is over. Nothing keeps you here."

Madame Chermidy resolutely seated herself on the stone bench as she said, "I shall not go till I have seen Don Diego."

"Don Diego !" the convalescent said. "You shall not see him ! I will not let you see him. Listen to me attentively, madame. I am still very weak, but I will find a lion's strength to defend my husband. It

is not that I doubt him ; he is good, he loves me as a
sister, and will soon love me as a wife.   But I do not
wish to have his heart distracted between past and
present ; it would be dreadful to condemn him to choose
between us.   Besides, you see that he has made his
choice as he no longer writes to you."

" Child ! you have not learned what love is in your
barley-water.   You know not the empire we assume
over a man when we have made him happy !   You
never saw what golden threads, finer and closer than
those of a spider's web, we weave about his heart.   I
have not come to declare war against . you without
arms ;   I bring with me the remembrance of three
years of passion, gratified and never satiated.   You are
at liberty to oppose to this your sisterly kisses and
schoolgirl caresses.   Perhaps you fancy you have extinguished the fire I kindled ?   Wait till I have blown
on it and you will see a grand conflagration."

" You shall not speak to him, even were he weak
enough to consent to this fatal interview ; his mother
and I will manage to prevent it."

" I care not for his mother !   I have claims on her
too, and I will prove them."

" I know not what claims a woman can have who
has behaved like you, but I know that the church and
the law gave the Count de Villanera to me, on the
same day as they gave me to him."

" Listen.   I leave you the entire disposition of all
the property you possess.   Live, be happy and rich :
cause the happiness of your family, nurse the old age
of your parents, but leave me Don Diego.   He is nothing

to you as yet, as you have just confessed; he is not your husband, he is only your physician, your nurse, the assistant of Dr. le Bris."

"He is everything to me, madame, since I love him."

"Ah! now we have it—come, let us change the key. Give me back my son. He is mine, at any rate; I hope you will not deny that : when I handed him over to you, I made my conditions. You have not kept your word, so I withdraw mine."

"Madame," Germaine replied, "if you really loved little Gomez, you would not dream of depriving him of his name and fortune."

"I do not care ; I love him for myself, as all mothers do. I would sooner have a bastard to kiss every morning than hear a Marquis call you mamma."

"I am aware," Germaine replied, "that the child was yours, but you gave him to me. You have no more right to reclaim him than I have to give him up to you."

"I will appeal to law. I will reveal the mystery of his birth. I run no risk now ; my husband is dead, so he cannot kill me."

"You will lose your cause."

"But I shall gain a glorious scandal. Ah! Madame de Villanera is punctilious about the honour of her name ! Infamous deeds have been done to render the name of the Villaneras illustrious. I will pillory this grand name which Italy disputes with Spain. I will move the trial from court to court : I will have it inserted in all the papers : I will amuse the public-houses of Paris with it, and the old Countess will burst with spite. The lawyers may say what they please, the judges do as they like ! I shall lose my trial; but all future Villaneras will have the Chermidy stain."

She spoke with so much heat that her language attracted the attention of the little Marquis. He was about ten yards from them, being engaged in planting branches in the sand, to make a little garden. He quitted his labour and planted himself before Madame Chermidy, with his fist thrust in his side. On seeing him approach Germaine said to the widow, " Passion must render you very forgetful, madame. For an hour you have been claiming this child, and never once thought of folding him to your heart !"

The Marquis offered his cheek with considerable reluctance, and then said to his terrible mother in th broken language of children of that age :

" What 'oo say to mamma ?"

" Marquis," Germaine replied, " this lady wants to take you to Paris. Will you go with her ?"

The boy's only reply was to throw himself into Germaine's arms, and cast an angry glance at Madame Chermidy.

" We all love him," Germaine said ; " you as well· That is clear."

" It is natural, he is so like his father." The widow said to her son, " Look at me ; do you not know me ?',

" No."

" I am your mother."

" No."

" You are my son—my son !"

" Not 'oo son ; mamma Germaine's son."

" Have you not another mother ?"

" Yes, I have mamma Nera. She is gone to mamma Vitré's."

" It seems that all the world is his mamma, save myself. Do you not remember me at Paris ?"

" What dat Paris ?"

" I gave you sugarplums."

" What sugarplums ?"

" Come, children are little men ; they cut ingratitude with their teeth. Marquis de los Montes de Hiero, listen to me. All these mammas are those who have brought you up, while I am your real mother, your only mother, the one who bore you."

The child understood nothing except that the lady was scolding him. He cried bitterly, and Germaine had difficulty in consoling him. " For see, madame," she said to the widow, " that no one keeps you here, not even the Marquis."

" I will tell you my final resolve," she replied, firmly. But a well-known voice interrupted her : it was Dr. le Bris, who had arrived from Corfu at full gallop. He had seen Lump at a window of the Trafalgar Hotel, and brought the grand news at full speed. Madame Chermidy's driver, whom he found at the door of the villa, caused him an awful alarm by telling him that he had brought a lady. He ran through the house, kicked up every servant he came across, and rushed down the garden steps at full speed.

The doctor did not think that Madame Chermidy was capable of a crime ; still, he breathed a sigh of

satisfaction on finding Germaine as he had left her.
He felt her pulse before anything else, and said,

" Countess, you are rather agitated, and I think that
solitude would be of great service to you. Be kind
enough to sit down, while I lead this lady back to her
carriage."

He gave this decree with a smile, but in such a tone
of authority that Madame Chermidy accepted his arm
without a reply.

When they had gone a little distance, he said to her,
" I hope, my lovely patient, that you do not intend to
undo my handiwork ? What on earth have you come
to seek here ?"

She replied, simply, " What letter did you write to
the old Duke ?"

" Ah ! I see ; in truth, we had a stormy week ; but
fine weather has returned."

" Is there no resource ; Key of Hearts ?"

" None, I am sorry to say."

" What do you gain by it ?"

" Only the satisfaction of doing my duty. It is a
famous cure, come : they are not to be counted by
dozens."

" My poor fellow, people say you will get on, but I
am afraid you will grovel all your life. Clever men are
sometimes very stupid."

" What can I do ? It is impossible to satisfy the
whole world."

" What will become of me ? I lose everything."

" Do you think so ?"

" Undoubtedly !"

"Do you count thousands as nothing? you are a woman of sense, you looked out for the solid."

"Are you expressing your own opinion?"

"Mine and some other persons'"

"Is Don Diego one of them?"

"Possibly."

"They are very unjust. For a trifle I would return him all he gave me."

"You are quite certain he would not accept it. Good-bye, madame."

"Is that Mathieux the Duke sent you from Paris still in your service?"

"Yes; why?"

"Because I told you to be on your guard against him."

"That was the very reason I prevented his being turned away."

Madame Chermidy returned hurriedly to town. This retreat strongly resembled a rout, and Lump, who was awaiting news at the window, guessed at the first glance that the battle-field had remained in the hands of the enemy. The widow rushed up-stairs, threw herself into an easy-chair, and said to her accomplice, "The day is lost!"

"Has she recovered?"

"She is cured!"

"The impudent creature! Did you see the Count?"

"No; they will hide him from me so cleverly that I shall not get at him. Le Bris almost turned me out of doors."

"If ever he gets a patient again may I lose my good name. And my little Jew—was he an ass?"

"Or a rogue.   He has cheated us like all the rest!"

"Who can one trust in, if we cannot put faith in a convict?   I suppose they have discharged him?"

"No; he is still there."

"Come, there is a chance!   You will not give in altogether?"

"Nonsense!   I must see Don Diego."

"We will find him for you."

"We will hire some cottage near the villa."

"Ah! if you ever get him to yourself, you will do anything you please with him : you are magnificent."

"It is my passion.   I claimed the child and threatened a lawsuit.   He will be afraid to come."

"If he comes you will carry him off?"

"Like a feather!"

"Perhaps you did wrong to speak about a trial, for he is too haughty to yield to that.   Attacking a Spaniard with threats is like stroking a wolf against the hair."

"If threats are of no use, I have another idea.   I will make a will in favour of the Marquis, leave him every farthing, and kill myself."

"Is that your scheme?   That will be a deal of use."

"What a goose you are!   I will kill myself without hurt.   The will will prove that I do not care for money—the knife will prove that I do not care for life.   But I shall not pretend to stab myself till he turns the handle of the door."

Lump considered the invention excellent, though not precisely novel.   "Good," she said; "he is a simple gentleman : he will not allow a woman he once loved to commit suicide for his sake. What asses men are ! If I had been as pretty as you I would have played them some tricks."

The next day the two women, escorted by a hired servant, proceeded to the south of the island. They found, near the Villa Dandolo, a pretty house for sale or lease, with a meadow. It was the one the dowager had chosen for the Duke, in case he came to spend the summer in Corfu, and it was also the castle in the air of poor Mantoux called *Littleluck.* The house was hired on the twenty-fourth, furnished on the twenty-fifth, occupied on the morning of the next day, and the news was speedily sent to Don Diego.

For three days the count had been in torture. Germaine told him of the visit she had received. The poor child did not know how he would receive the news, and yet she wished to break it to him herself. In announcing to Don Diego the arrival of his former mistress she assured herself in a moment if he were really cured of his love. A man taken by surprise has not the time to prepare his face, and the first impression that appears on it is the true one. Germaine played for a heavy stake in subjecting her husband to such a trial, for a glance of joy in the count's eyes would have killed her more surely than a pistol-ball. But women are made so, and their heroic love prefers a sure danger to uncertain happiness.

The count was thoroughly cured ; for he heard the news with evident dissatisfaction ; his brow was clouded by a sorrow not at all exaggerated, because it was sincere. He did not seem either outraged or scandalized ; for Madame Chermidy's behaviour, though impertinent in the eyes of all the rest, was excusable for him. He did not put on the grimace of the governor of a province who hears that the enemy has effected a descent upon his shores ; but he evinced the chagrin of a man whose felicity a foreseen accident has arrived to trouble.

Germaine could not repeat to him without some degree of anger the insolent remarks of this woman and her monstrous pretensions. The doctor joined in chorus with her ; and the old countess openly regretted that she had not been there to throw the creature into the sea or out of the door. But Don Diego, instead of espousing the quarrel of the whole family, applied himself to soothe anger and dress wounds. He defended his old mistress, or rather pitied her, as a gentleman who no longer loves, but flatters himself that he is still loved. He performed this duty with such delicacy that Germaine admired him for it, as she appreciated once again the rectitude and firmness of his mind. She allowed him to bestow his pity on Madame Chermidy, because she was quite sure she had his whole love.

The dowager was far less tolerant, for the claim to the boy and the threat of a scandalous trial exasperated her. She spoke of nothing less than handing the widow over to the magistrates, and having her disgracefully expelled as an adventuress. " Mr. Stevens is our friend," she said ; " he will not refuse us this slight service." She considered that the visit of

Madame Chermidy to Germaine bore all the character
of an attempted murder, for the presence of so veno-
mous a creature was enough to kill a convalescent.
And the doctor did not say no.

The count tried to calm his mother. "Do not be
alarmed," he said ; "she will bring no trial ; she is
not so unnatural as to compromise her son at the same
time as us. Anger doubtlessly led her astray. It's
easy for us who are happy to speak sensibly ; but she
must be indignant with me, and regard me as a great
villain, for I abandoned her without any cause of reproach. I have not written a line to her in eight
mouths, and have given my whole soul to another.
She would be still more angry with me if she knew
that the happiest days of my life are those I spent far
from her and near Germaine, or if I were to tell her
that my heart is full of love up to the brim, like those
goblets which one drop more would make run over.
Let me dismiss her with kind words. Why should I
not go and open my heart to her, and show her there
is no room left for her ? It only needs one hour of
gentleness and firmness to change this embittered love
into pure and durable friendship. She will no longer
dream of making a scandal ; she will remain worthy to
meet us in society, and to inquire at times after her
son. There are few women who do not run the risk
of elbowing in society some ex-mistress of their husbands, still they do not pluck out each other's eyes ;
past and present live happily together, so soon as the
frontier that separates them is distinctly traced. Consider, besides, that our situation is rather exceptional.

Whatever we may do, whatever that unhappy woman may do, she will still be in the sight of God the mother of our child.   If she had only been its nurse, we should consider it our duty to insure her against wretchedness ; then let us not refuse to take an innocent and prudent step which may save her from despair and crime."

Don Diego spoke with such good faith that Germaine offered him her hand, and said, " I told that woman she should never see you again ; but had I then heard you speak with so much reason and experience I would have fetched you myself and taken you to her.   Order the carriage without loss of time ; run and say farewell to her, and pardon her the ill she has done me as freely as I pardon her."

" Very fine !" the Countess Dowager said ; " but if he were to get into the carriage I would unharness the horses with my own hand.   Don Diego, you did not consult me when you took a mistress ; you did not listen to me when I told you you had fallen into the clutches of an intriguer.   But, as you consult me to-day, you must hear me to the end.   I arranged your marriage ; I suffered you, on behalf of the family, to form a bargain, which would be odious among the middle classes ; but the greatness of the interest in-volved, and the principle to be saved, excuse much. Heaven has allowed an affair, begun so badly, to turn out well ; but it shall never be said that, during my lifetime, you left your holy and legitimate wife to go to your old mistress.   I am well aware you no longer love her, but you do not despise her sufficiently for me to consider you cured. This Chermidy had you for three years in her clutches, and I will not let you run the risk of falling into them again. You may shake your head, my son, but the flesh is weak. I know it from your case, if not from my own. I am acquainted with men, although I had never one to pay court to me. But when a woman has been at the play for fifty years, she may be allowed to know something of the plot ; and remember this : the best of men is not worth a dump, and you may consider yourself the best of men if you like. You are cured of your love, but these parasitic amours belong to the family of the acacia. You pull up the tree and burn the roots, but yet scions spring up by thousands. Who can guarantee me that the sight of this woman will not make you lose your head ? for your brain is not strong enough to bear such a shock. A man who has once drunk will drink, and you drank so heavily that people thought you drowned in liquor. If you had been married three or four years, if you were living the life you will soon lead, if the marquis had a brother or a sister, I might, perhaps, relax the bridle. But, supposing that your madness were to come on again, I should have done a pretty thing in marrying you to our angel. For these reasons, my dear count, you will not go to Madame Chermidy's, even to say good-bye to her ; and if you choose to go against my will, you will not find your mother or wife here on your return."

Don Diego could say nothing in reply, but he felt ill at ease for several days. M. le Bris changed his patient, and took care of his friend's mind. He tried

to uproot the obstinate illusions the count still yielded
to as regarded his mistress, and he pitilessly broke all
the pieces of coloured glass which the poor gentleman
had allowed to be placed before his eyes. He told
him all he knew about the lady's past history; he
showed her to him; ambitious, greedy, cunning, in
fact, such as she was. "I am called the tomb of secrets,"
the doctor thought, while unpacking his budget of
scandal, "but justice has the right to open tombs."
He saw that Don Diego still doubted, so he made him
read the last letter he had received from Madame
Chermidy. The count was seized with horror at
finding in it a hint at assassination, for which a reward
of twenty thousand pounds was held out.

The duke arrived upon this, and furnished a living
proof of Madame Chermidy's criminality. The poor
old gentleman had travelled without accident, thanks
to that instinct of self-preservation we have in common
with the brutes : but his mind had dropped all its
ideas on the road, like a necklace of beads of which the
string is broken. He managed to find the Villa
Dandolo, and dropped in on the astonished family
with no more emotion than if he had just left his
bedroom. Germaine leaped on his neck and smothered
him in caresses, and he endured them like a dog, that
affords amusement to a child.

"How kind and good you are !" she said to him.
" You knew my danger and came hurrying to me."

" Stay, let me see ; you are not dead, then ? how
have you settled matters ? I am very pleased at it—
that is, not extremely ; and Honorine is furious with

you. Is she not here ? she came to marry Villanera—
if she would only pardon me."

It was impossible to get a word from him as to the
Duchess' health ; but he spoke of Honorine as much
as they liked. He described all the happiness and
wretchedness she had caused him ; all his conversation
turned on her, all his questions related to her : he
wished to see her at any price, and he displayed the craft
of an Indian savage to discover Honorine's address.

The poor old man's unexpected arrival was a serious
grief to Germaine and a cruel lesson for Don Diego.
The Dowager, who never had any sympathy for the
Duke, took but slight interest in the ruin of his intellect,
but she triumphed at having in her power a victim of
Madame Chermidy's. She attached herself closely to the
poor old Duke ; she dragged from him all the secrets of
his wretchedness and his decadence, and she continually
turned the handle of this cracked instrument, whose
music was sweet to her maternal ears.

The Duke had been mooning about the house for
some hours, when Madame Chermidy sent to let Don
Diego know that she was his neighbour, and expecting
him. The Count showed the letter to M. le Bris.

"What reply would you give, in my place ?" he said,
shrugging his shoulders.

" I would offer her money. She came here to take
your name, person, and fortune ; when she saw that
the Countess was not dead she resigned the first and
fell back on the other two. When she sees that she
will have to resign the second too, she will be satisfied
with money."

"But this trial, the scandal she threatens us with !"

"Offer her money."

"But her son !"

"Money, I tell you; of course it must be a good round sum. You give a penny to a man who begs in his shirt sleeves, a shilling to the man who has a coat, and five to a man who wears a suit of black ; now, calculate how much you must offer one who begs in a coach and four."

"Will you go and see what she wants ?"

"Of course. You hired me by the month, so the visits are not counted."

The doctor proceeded to Madame Chermidy's. When he entered he found her prepared for a scene ; seated languishingly in a large chair, with pendant arms and unloosed hair, she looked like Niobe all tears.

"Good day, madame," the doctor said ; "pray don't disturb yourself, it is only I."

She sprang up and ran to him, saying :

"Is it you, my friend ? You caused me great pain the other day—ought you to have received me in such a way after so long a parting ?"

"Do not talk about that, pray. I have not come as a friend, but as an envoy."

"Shall I not see him, then ?"

"No ; but if you are anxious to see anybody, I can show you the Duke."

"What, is he here ?"

"Since the morning—a pretty object you have made of him."

" I am not responsible for all the old fools who lose their heads for me."

"Nor for the thousands they lose at your house. Granted !"

" In good faith, Key of Hearts, do you believe that I am a woman of money ?"

"Massive ! how much do you want to return to Paris and keep quiet ?"

" Nothing."

" Your passage will be paid, even if it cost ten thousand pounds."

" There are two of us : I brought Lump."

"The sum may be doubled."

" What would you gain by that ? If I am what you suppose, I would take the money to-day and make a disturbance to-morrow. But I am worth more than all of you."

" Much obliged !"

" Stay, handsome ambassador. Carry this to the king, your master, and tell him that if he has any commissions for the next world, he can send them to me this evening."

" What ! extreme measures so soon ?"

" Yes, my friend ; there is my last will and testament. The parcel is not sealed : you can read it."

He read :

" ' On the point of voluntarily quitting a life which the desertion of Count de Villanera has rendered hateful to me ——'

" Naughty woman !" the Doctor said, breaking off his reading.

"It is the pure truth."

"Oblige me by omitting that sentence.   In the first place it is not grammatical."

"Women only write letters well : they have no speciality for wills."

"Well, then, I proceed :"

" ' I, Honorine Lavenaze, Widow Chermidy, being of sound mind and body, bequeath all my estates, funded property, &c., without reserve, to Gomez, Marquis de los Montes de Hierro, only son of the Count de Villanera, my old lover !   Signed, sealed, and delivered, and so on.'   And it will come into operation to-morrow."

"I believe not."

"You defy me ?"

"Certainly."

"And why should I not kill myself, if you please ?"

"Because it would cause too much pleasure to three or four honest people of my acquaintance.   Good-bye madame."

The door had hardly closed on the Doctor, when Lump came from an adjoining room, accompanied by Mantoux.

CHAPTER XIII.

PLAYING WITH EDGED TOOLS.

MATHIEU MANTOUX could not console himself for the recovery of Germaine. He accused the druggist of having sold him adulterated arsenic, a very forgery of poison. In his grief he neglected his duties and wandered dreamily about the villa, the object of his walk being ever that pretty little property of which he had once hoped to be lord. Through continually looking at it, he knew the minutest details about it, just as if he had been brought up there from the earliest age ; he knew how many windows the house had, and there was not a tree in the garden which did not remind him of something. He had entered the grounds more than once : indeed, it was a matter of no great difficulty, for though this earthly paradise was surrounded by a hedge of cactus and aloes, a formidable defence if carefully looked after, three or four aloes had blossomed in the month of August, and the flower kills the plant. Thus, the impenetrable barrier had fallen at several places, and Mantoux's livery easily forced its way through, without fear of being torn.

On the 26th of September, about four in the afternoon, this melancholy scamp was dreaming of his ill-luck as he walked along the hedge. He thought with a bitter sweetness of his first interview with Lump, and

Madame Chermidy's obliging reception. When he compared his present situation with that he had dreamed of, he found himself the most unhappy of men : for we are apt to regard that as lost which we have all but gained. The apparition of an enormous mass moving heavily about the garden interrupted the course of his ideas : he rubbed his eyes and asked himself whether he saw Lump or her shadow : but he remembered that shadows do not have so much substance. Lump saw him, and made him a sign to come to her : she was thinking at the very moment of the best way of getting at him.

"Hilloh !" she said; "it's you, is it, the excellent nurse? You took good care of your mistress—she is cured."

He replied with an enormous sigh, "I never had any luck."

"We are alone," Lump went on ; "no one can hear us, and there is no time to lose. Are you pleased at seeing your mistress in such good health ?"

"Certainly, miss ; and yet your lady promised me something else."

"What did she promise you ?"

"That my lady would soon die, and I should have a pension of £60 a year."

"You would have liked that better, I suppose ?"

"Why ! I should have been my own master, instead of serving others for the rest of my days."

"And you never thought of giving the disease a help-hand ?"

Mantoux looked at her with evident trouble : he did

not know whether he had to do with a judge or an accomplice. But she helped him from the dilemma by adding, "I know you : I saw you at Toulon. When I unearthed you at Corbeil I knew your history."

" Oh, then, you are in the swim. You had a reason for sending me here ?"

" Of course : if I had not had work to do, I should have chosen an honest man. There are enough of them, perhaps too many."

" That's the meaning of the pension, is it ?"

" Of course."

" I'll bet, then, that you wrote me the anonymous letter."

" Who else could it be ?"

" But what interest have you in it ?"

" Why, your mistress stole my mistress's husband. Now do you understand ?"

" I'm beginning to do so."

" You ought to have begun sooner, you ass."

" I did not understand, I allow, and yet I worked."

" With what ?"

" I bought some arsenic, and she took some every night."

" On your word ?"

" On my *honour !*"

" You did not give her enough."

" I was afraid of being caught ; it's found in dead bodies."

" You coward !"

" Oh! I should like to know who would have his neck stretched for £60 a year !"

"My lady would have given you as much as you wanted."

"You ought to have told me so; now it is too late."

"It is never too late; come and speak to my lady."

Mantoux waited for the Doctor's departure in a room opening out of the saloon : a few words of the conversation reached his ear, but for all that, he only half comprehended the bargain about to be made with him. He approached Madame Chermidy with respectful distrust, and the widow did not think it advisable to enter into explanations with him until she had received an answer from Don Diego. She was greatly agitated, and walked up and down the saloon repeatedly : she listened to Lump without hearing her, and looked at the convict without seeing him. The courtesy of Count de Villanera was sufficiently well known to her for her to see in his absence and silence alarming symptoms.

"He no longer loves me, then," she thought ; "I would not mind about indifference, for I could soon warm up his coldness. But I must have been blackened in his eyes : he must have been told everything, and he despises me ! Were it not for that he would never have treated me thus. To offer me money through that odious le Bris ! and in what terms ! If he regard me with the same eyes as his ambassador, it is all over with me : he will never come back again. Widower or not, he is lost to me. Then, what good would simple vengeance : well, be it so ; I will avenge myself. But we will wait : if he does not hasten here as soon as he has received my message, it is because all is lost."

" I beg your pardon, madame," Mantoux interrupted her; " I must go and serve my dinner, and if your ladyship has any orders to give me —— "

" Go and serve your dinner," she said ; "you are in my service. Listen carefully to all that is said, and repeat it to me."

" Yes, madame."

" Wait a moment ! perhaps M. de Villanera will come himself during the evening, and if so I shall not want you. Still, hang about here till the morning—if he were not to pay me a visit—but it is impossible. You will run here as soon as he has gone to bed. No matter about the hour : Lump may be asleep, but do you ring, and I will let you in."

" It is not necessary, madame, when a man has been a locksmith—besides, I have my tools still."

" Well, I will wait ; but I feel sure the Count will come."

Mantoux served at table, but though he kept his ears wide open, the name of Madame Chermidy even was not once pronounced. It was a family dinner, with only one stranger, Mr. Stevens. The old Countess asked him whether the English law allowed magistrates to expel adventurers without any other form of trial ; and he replied that the legislature of his country protected individual liberty even in its abuses.

The Doctor said with a smile, " Very good, so far ; and now about lady adventurers ?"

" They are treated rather more severely."

"Even when they have a fortune of a quarter of a million, say ?"

"If you know many of that sort, Doctor, send them all to England ; they will be crowned with roses there, and marry lords."

The Dowager made a face, and turned the conversation.

During the whole meal the aged Duke kept his eyes fixed on Mantoux's face. His poor forgetful brain managed to recognise a man he had seen but once at Madame Chermidy's. He took him on one side after the dessert, and led him mysteriously to his bedroom.

"Where is she ?" he said. "You know where she is hidden, for they are hiding her from me."

"My lord," he replied, "I do not know of whom―― "

"I am speaking of Honorine, you know. Honorine —the lady in Paris at whose house I saw you."

"Madame Chermidy ?"

"Ah ! I was certain you knew her, and that you have seen her. My daughter has seen her too, so has the Doctor, everybody but me. Go and find her, and I will make your fortune."

And the truthful Mantoux replied, "I can swear to your lordship that I do not know where Madame Chermidy is."

"Tell me at once, you scoundrel ! I will not mention it to a soul ; it shall be a secret between us two ; but," he added, in a menacing tone, "if you do not lead me to her this evening, I will have your head cut off."

The convict trembled, as if the old man could read his soul.   But the duke had already changed his key; he was crying.

"My lad," he said, "I have no secrets from you, and I must tell you the misfortune that threatens us. Honorine means to kill herself this evening. She told the doctor so, and she has sent her will to my son-in-law. They pretend she will not do it, and only wanted to frighten us, but I know her better than all of them. She will certainly kill herself, and why should she not? She has killed me who am now speaking to you. Did you notice that large knife on her mantelpiece in Paris? She thrust it into my heart one day. I can well remember it. She will stab herself with the same knife to-night, if I do not find her in time. Will you lead me to her?"

Mantoux protested that he did not know the lady's address, but he could not persuade the old madman. Up till ten o'clock the duke followed him everywhere, into the garden, pantry, kitchen, with the patience of a savage. "You can do as you like," he said to himself, "but you will be obliged to go to her, and I will follow you."

People go to bed at an early hour in the Ionian Islands, and by midnight the whole house slept, save the duke and Mantoux. The convict crept downstairs without a sound, but in crossing the north garden he fancied he saw a shadow glide through the olive trees. He struck out into the fields and crept along the hedges, by winding paths, to the house he knew so well. The obstinate shadow followed him in the distance, up to the hedge before the cottage, and he asked himself if he was not the victim of an hallucination : he mustered up his courage, however, turned back and looked for the enemy ; the road was deserted, and the apparition lost in the darkness.

A profound obscurity veiled the cottage ; the only window illumined was that of Madame Chermidy on the ground-floor, and Mantoux understood that he was expected. He unrolled a bundle of skeleton keys he had wrapped in linen to deaden the sound of the iron, but he had not time to set to work before Madame Chermidy opened the door. "Speak low," she said, "Lump has just gone to sleep."

The two accomplices entered the room, and the first object that attracted Mantoux's eyes was the dagger of which the duke had spoken to him.

"Well," the widow said ; "has the count retired to bed ?"

" Yes, madame."

" The wretch ! what did they say at dinner ?"

" They did not mention your name."

" Not a word about me ?"

" No ! but after dinner the duke asked me for your address. I found him much altered."

"Did he say nothing else ?"

" Some nonsense—that you were about to kill yourself, and had made your will."

" I said so and wrote so, to force the count to come and see me. Is he gone to bed ?"

"Oh certainly, madame. His lordship's room is

close to ours, on the little back corridor.   The duke
put out his candle at eleven o'clock."

" Listen :. if they said any harm of me at the
table, pray repeat it without fear ; I shall not be
vexed—on the contrary, feel pleased."

" They did not once open their mouths about you."

" What ! I told them I was going to commit suicide
this night, and they did not even take the trouble to
say it was a happy release !"

" They paid no more attention to you, than if you
did not exist."

" Well : I will remind them that I am alive.   Lump
tells me that you gave the countess arsenic."

" Yes, but it did not act."

" Suppose you were to give her a knife, that would
act, perhaps ?"

" Oh, madame ! a knife—that would be a dangerous
matter."

" What difference is there ?"

" In the first place, madame, the countess was ill
and illness has a good broad back.   But to kill a person
in good health ! that is heavy work."

" You shall be paid for your trouble."

" And suppose I am caught ?"

" Find a boat, and go to Turkey ; the police will not
follow you so far."

" But I wanted to stay here ; I wished to buy some
property."

" Land costs nothing in Turkey."

" No matter.   What your ladyship desires is worth
two thousand pounds."

" Two thousand pounds !"

" Oh ! I trust you are not going to beat me down!"

" Be it so then—it is a bargain."

" And ready money ?"

"On the nail."

" Have you it with you ? for if you did not pay me the sum, I could not conveniently go to Paris to fetch it."

" I have five thousand pounds in my box."

" Grant me five minutes' reflection."

" Reflect !"

Mantoux turned to the mantelpiece, mechanically took up Madame Chermidy's Corsican dagger, and felt the point on his nail. Madame Chermidy was not even looking at him ; she was awaiting the result of his deliberations.

" I have it," he said; " I would rather stay here than go to Turkey, because our people are better treated at Corfu. Then, I have learned a little Italian, and shall never learn Turkish ; and, lastly, the house and garden you have hired suit me so exactly."

" But how on earth will you—"

" I have an excellent plan—instead of killing my mistress, I shall kill you. In the first place, I receive five thousand pounds instead of two thousand pounds. Secondly, no one will think of accusing me, as you made your will, and promised to commit suicide this night. You will be found on your bed, stabbed with your own dagger, and it will be seen that you are a woman of your word. Lastly, allow me to say, without meaning any offence, that I would sooner kill a profligate woman like you, than an honourable lady like my mistress, who has always treated me well. It is a first step I am going to try in the path of virtue, and I trust that the God of Abraham and of Jacob will reward me for doing His work."

* * * * * *

CHAPTER XIV.

THE WAGES OF SIN.

THE shadow which had followed Mantoux from the Villa Dandolo to Madame Chermidy's garden was the duke.

An instinct as infallible as reason told the madman that Mathieu was awaited by Madame Chermidy. He watched for his departure, and he stayed until the right moment at the end of a dark passage. When he heard the convict open his bedroom door, he managed to stifle his voice and compress the nervous laugh which shook his old body from head to foot. He was careful to take off his boots, so as to descend the stairs unnoticed by his guide, and walked the whole distance in his stockings over pebbles, sharp grass, and through thorns which rendered his very footstep bloody. He neither noticed the length of the road, nor fatigue, nor pain; the empire of a fixed idea rendered him insensible to everything; he feared nothing in the world but missing his guide, or being noticed by him. When Mantoux redoubled his speed, the duke ran behind him, as if he had wings. When the convict turned his head, the duke fell on his stomach, crept along ditches, or hid himself behind a thorny hedge of cactus or pomegranate.

Although he stopped at the hedge surrounding the cottage, a secret voice told him that the only window from which a light shone on the ground-floor was that of Madame Chermidy's room. He saw his conductor stop at the door; a female came to open it, and his old heart bounded with disordered joy on recognising the creature that attracted him.

She was not dead, then; he would see her, speak to her, and perhaps attach her once more to life! His first movement was to rush towards her, but he restrained himself; he felt sure that she would not kill herself in the presence of the domestic, and he determined to wait till she was alone, ere he rushed into her house, surprised her, and tore the dagger from her grasp.

He remained in hiding for a long hour, without noticing the departure of time. He loved Madame Chermidy as he had never loved wife or daughter; he felt ideas of devotion, abnegation, disinterested attentions, and humble slavery germinating in his brain. This absolute, unreflecting, unmeasured, and unlimited love was not a new sentiment with him, for he had loved himself in this way for sixty years. His egotism had changed its object but not its character; he was ready to sacrifice the whole world to a caprice of Madame Chermidy, as before to his own interests or pleasures.

Since the day the ungrateful woman quitted him, he had not loved; his heart could only beat near her, his lungs only breathed in the atmosphere she had inhaled. He passed through the world like an inert body launched into vacuum.

At times a gleam of reason crossed his mind, and he

R

said to himself, " I am an old madman—why do I talk
of love ? In fact, love sits well on an old dotard of my
age.   If she grant me a little friendship, I shall have
all I deserve.   If she will endure me in her house as a
father, I shall find paternal feelings in a nook of my
heart.   She is unhappy, she laments Villanera's
desertion ; I will console her with kind words."   The
hope of seeing her caused him a fever ; his eyes worn
with sleeplessness pained him terribly, but he hoped he
should weep when he fell at Honorine's feet.   The
duke, seated in a corner of the garden, opposite the
house, resembled an animal which has run for three
days across a desert in search of water, and now
halts before its last leaps, in front of the coveted
fountain, with haggard eye and pendent tongue.

The last candle was extinguished in the house, and
the window he watched faded away into darkness like
the others.   But the house, invisible to an indifferent
observer, was not so to the duke, and the window he
longed to approach shone like a sun before his inflamed
eyes.   He saw Mantoux come out of the house and fly
across the fields at headlong speed, without turning to
look back ; and then he quitted his hiding place, and
crept up to the window, which his eyes had not once
turned from.   He did not even think of going to try
if the door was fast, so much did this window possess
him !   He leaned on the sill, he felt the woodwork and
frame, he thrust his face against the panes, to which he
pressed his nose and mouth, and refreshed his torrid lips
by the contact with the glass.

The silence of night reigned within and without, but

the sickly senses of the old man fancied they could see Madame Chermidy kneeling at the foot of her bed, with her head buried in her hand, and her rosy lips parted in prayer. To attract her attention to him, he tapped gently on the window ; but no one replied. Then he thought he could see her asleep, for the most contradictory hallucinations succeeded each other in his brain. He reflected for a long time on a way of approaching her without startling or arousing her, and to gain his end he felt capable of anything, even of pulling down the wall with no other instruments than his fingers. While passing his hand over the window, he felt that the panes were set in leadwork, and he set about removing one with his nails. He worked with such a will that he at length succeeded ; his nails were repeatedly bent back or broken on the glass, his fingers were all bleeding, but he paid no attention to it ; and if he stopped every now and then, it was merely to lick the blood from his fingers and listen whether Honorine were still asleep.

When the square of glass was thus partly unfastened, he pushed it gently by the end, and gradually loosened it, stopping every time that the glass cracked a little, or a violent pull shook the whole window. At length his patience was rewarded : the transparent pane remained in his hand. He laid it noiselessly on the sand of the walk, gave a bound as he laid his finger on his lips, and inhaled the atmosphere of the room through the opening he had made. He expanded his chest with eager delight, for it was the first time he had breathed for ten days.

He thrust his hand into the room, felt the inside of
the window, and caught hold of the bolt. The panes
were small, the orifice was narrow, the lead cut his arm
and impeded his movements; still the window gave
way and creaked on its hinges. The duke was terrified
at the sound, and fancied all was lost; he fled to the
bottom of the garden and clambered up a tree, with his
eyes fixed on the house, his ears open to the slightest
sound. He listened for a long time, and heard nothing
but the gentle and melancholy croaking of the frogs
along the road; then he came down from his observa-
tory, and crawled on hands and knees to the window,
at one moment lowering his head not to be seen, at
another raising it both to see and hear. He returned
to the spot whence fear had driven him, and assured
himself that Honorine still slept.

The window was wide open and no longer creaked;
the night breeze entered the room without awaking the
lovely sleeper. The duke clambered through by the
window and crept noiselessly along the room, joy and
fear making him tremble like a tree shaken by the
wind. He tottered on his feet, but did not venture to
hold on by any article of furniture. The room was
encumbered with property of every description, trunks
open and closed, and even upset furniture. The duke
steered through these impediments with infinite pre-
caution, gliding along past every object without touching it, and thrusting his wounded hands forth into the
darkness. At each step he took he murmured in a low
voice, "Honorine, are you there, do you hear me? It
is I, your old friend, the most unhappy but most

respectful of your friends. Be not alarmed, fear nothing, not even that I shall reproach you. I was mad at Paris, but the voyage has altered me. I am a father come to console you. Do not kill yourself, for it would kill me !"

He stopped, was silent and listened, but he heard nothing save the beating of his own heart. He felt afraid, and sat down on the ground to calm his emotion and the boiling of his blood.

"Honorine!" he exclaimed, as he rose, "are you dead?" It was death in person that replied to him : he stumbled against an article of furniture and his hands swam in a pool of blood.

He fell on his knees, rested his head on the bed, and remained in the same position till daybreak. He never asked himself how this misfortune had happened; he felt neither surprise nor regret; the blood flowed to his brain, and all was over. His head was only an open cage whence reason had fled : he passed the last hours of the night resting on a corpse, which was gradually turning cold.

When Lump came to see whether her cousin were awake, she heard through the door a shrill and dis-cordant cry like the croak of a raven. She saw a blood-dripping old man, who shook his head as if desirous to hurl it from him, and who incessantly repeated "Aca ! aca ! aca !"—it was all left to the duke of the gift of speech, that finest privilege of humanity. His face grimaced horribly; his eyes opened and shut as if moved by springs ; his legs were paralysed, his body nailed to the chair, his hands dead.

Lump had never known but one human feeling, adoration for her mistress ; it is the lot of poor relations to attach themselves furiously to their family, either in love or hatred. The enormous woman threw herself on the body of her mistress with a cry the like of which could only be heard in the desert ; she bewailed her as tigresses must mourn over their whelps. She tore the knife from a large gaping wound that no longer bled ; she raised in her arms the lovely inanimate corpse, and covered it with maddened caresses. If souls could be divided, she would have resuscitated her dear Honorine at her own expense. But rage soon succeeded to grief, and Lump did not for a moment doubt that the duke was the assassin. She threw the body on the bed, and fell with her entire weight on the duke ; she struck him, she bit him, she tried to tear his eyes out. But the duke was insensible to physical pain ; he replied to all these assaults by that uniform cry which would henceforth be his only language. Animals have different sounds to express joy or pain ; but man attacked by paralytic madness is at the lowest scale of creation. Lump was weary of beating him before he began to suspect that he was being struck.

In the meanwhile, Germaine, fair and smiling as the morn, had awakened her mother and husband, seen the child dressed, and gone down into the garden to breathe the balmy air of autumn. The doctor and Mr. Stevens soon joined her there. The sea-breeze was gently caressing the leaves that glistened with dew ; the beautiful oranges and enormous lemons swung at the end of the green stalks; the wrinkled jujubes and pistachio nuts fell with a resounding noise at the foot of the trees; the olives stained the pale leaves of the olive-trees black; the heavy clusters of yellow grapes hung along the trellises; the figs of the second crop distilled honey in large drops; and some forgotten pomegranates smiled amid the foliage like those chubby nymphs of Virgil who conceal themselves that they may be better seen. The season of flowers was past, but the fine yellow and red fruits are the fragrant flowers of autumn, and the eyes rejoice to gaze on them.

The whole family was assembled round little Gomez, who was teasing a tame tortoise; the only absentee being the duke, whose windows were still closed, and his sleep was respected. Mathieu Mantoux, who had redoubled his zeal since the doctor had kept him in his place, was washing his linen on the bank of a small stream that ran down to the sea.

Mr. Stevens's servant came in all haste to summon his master; a crime had been committed in the vicinity; all the village was in alarm, and they ran to the judge at once. Mr. Stevens, in excusing himself to his friends, asked the messenger for some details.

"I know nothing," the man replied. "I hear it is a French lady found dead in her bed."

"Close here?" the doctor interrupted.

"About half a mile off."

"Did you hear whether she was a new arrival?"

"I believe so; but her maid only talks French, and no one could understand her."

" You saw the servant—a stout woman ?"

" Enormous !"

" That will do," M. le Bris said. " My dear Mr. Stevens, there is the breakfast-bell, and, if you believe me, you will come and sit down. The dead woman is quite well, I will guarantee you."

Mr. Stevens did not understand a joke, and the doctor added : " Does the English law punish people who promise to commit suicide and do not keep their word ?"

" No ! but it punishes suicide when it is proved."

" Well ! I cannot get on with that English law !"

Mr. Stevens continued : " Seriously, doctor, have you any reason for believing in a false alarm ?"

" I give you my word that the lady has not received a scratch. I know her well, and she is too sweet on her white skin to make holes in it."

" But suppose she has been assassinated ?"

" Do not believe it, my excellent friend. Are you anything of a naturalist ?"

" Not much."

" Then you do not know the difference between the blue-headed and black-headed tomtit ?"

" No !"

" The blue-heads are dear little innocent creatures that allow themselves to be killed without any resistance, while the black-heads are the assassins. Now the lady in question is a black-headed tomtit."

" I do not understand you," Mr. Stevens said. " Why was I sent for, then ?"

" Most subtle judge, if you were sent for, it was not

for the pleasure of having a chat with you. It was to attract another person, who will not disturb himself. What do you say, dear count ?"

"He is right," said the dowager.

The count made no reply, for he was more affected than he would like to be seen. Germaine offered him her hand, and said, "Go with Mr. Stevens, and let us hope that the doctor is a true prophet."

"Confuse it," the doctor said ; "then I shall go too, though no one did me the politeness to invite me. But, if the lady be not hopelessly dead, I swear by my diploma that the count shall not say a word to her."

Mr. Stevens, the count, and the doctor got into a carriage, and in ten minutes stopped before Madame Chermidy's house. As soon as they could see it, the doctor changed his opinion, and thought that some misfortune had happened. A compact crowd was assembled, and the Maltese policeman, who had hurried up at the news of the count, could hardly keep them back.

"Hang it all !" M. le Bris said to himself, "has the little lady really killed herself to play us a trick ? I did not think her so strong-minded as that."

M. de Villanera was gnawing his moustaches without saying a word : he had loved Madame Chermidy for three years, and had believed himself sincerely loved, and his heart was lacerated by the thought that she had killed herself for him. The reminiscences of the past revolted against all the doctor's assurances, and victoriously pleaded Honorine's cause.

The crowd opened a passage to Mr. Stevens and his

companions, and under the escort of the police they entered the chamber of death. Madame Chermidy was lying on her bed in the dress she had worn on the previous evening : her lovely face was contracted by a horrible pang, and her half-opened lips displayed two rows of little teeth clenched in the last convulsion of death. Her eyes, which a pious hand had not closed in time, seemed to gaze on death with terror. The dagger was in the middle of the room where Lump had thrown it, and the blood had poured over her clothes, the sheets, the furniture, and everywhere. A large glazed pool before the mantelpiece announced that the unhappy woman had been struck there, and a dark-red track showed that she had possessed strength enough to walk as far as the bed.

The waiting woman, who had summoned the police, and aroused the neighbourhood, no longer uttered a sound : it seemed as if she had expended her fury in exhausting her strength. Cowering in a corner of the room, with her eyes fixed on the corpse of her mistress, she saw the man of law move backwards and forwards. Even the arrival of the count and Dr. le Bris did not arouse her from her torpor.

Mr. Stevens carefully examined the state of the room, and dictated the description of the corpse with the impassiveness of justice. The doctor, being requested to assist the inquiry, began by stating all he knew, shortly explained the causes which might have induced Madame Chermidy to kill herself, repeated the conversation he had with her, and recited the will he had carried himself to the count. The statements of the deceased woman, the place where the body was found, the doors of the house shut, the weapon having belonged to her, and, lastly, the vicinity of the waiting woman, who heard no sound—all these proved facts confirmed the idea of a suicide.

This word pronounced in a whisper had the effect of an electric shock upon Lump : she jumped up, ran to the doctor, looked him in the face, and shrieked, " Suicide ! did you say suicide ? You know very well she was not the woman to kill herself ! Poor angel ! She had such a happy life ! She was in such splendid health ! She would have lived a hundred years if you had not assassinated her. Besides, why is not the old villain here ? where have you put him ? Go and look at him, or have him here : you will see he is all covered with her blood !" She then noticed the Count de Villanera, who had sunk on a chair, and was silently weeping. " At last you are here, then !" she said to him : " you should have come sooner. Ah, my lord ! you have a strange way of paying your love debts !"

While the judge and the doctor proceeded to the next room, where a painful surprise awaited them, Lump dragged the count to the bedside, forced him to look at his former mistress, and listen to a funeral harangue which made his hair stand on end. " See ! see !" she said, amid her sobs; " look at those lovely eyes that smiled on you so tenderly, that pretty mouth that gave you such sweet kisses, those long black tresses, which you liked so to unfasten ! Do you remember the first time you came to our house ? when all had left, you fell on your knees to kiss that hand ; but how cold it is! And do you remember the day her boy was born? Who laughed then? who swore fidelity till death? Kiss her, then, faithful knight."

The count, motionless, rigid, and colder than the corpse he was gazing on, expiated in one moment three years of illegitimate happiness.

The duke was then brought in, who paid, and very dearly, for a life of egotism and ingratitude.

The blood with which he was covered, his presence at Madame Chermidy's, the pane missing from the window, the scratches on his hands, and, above all, the loss of reason, caused it to be believed for an instant that he was the assassin. The doctor examined the wound, and found that it passed entirely through the heart : hence, death must have been instantaneous, and it was impossible for the victim to have dragged herself to the bed. Mr. Stevens, while dining with the duke on the previous evening, noticed how much his intellect was weakened, and the doctor explained in a few words how a homicidal monomania might have germinated in a single night in this deranged brain. Even if he had committed the crime, justice could have no dealings with a madman : nature had condemned him to a speedy death, after a few months of an existence worse than death.

But, on examining the corpse more closely, there were found, in her clenched hand, a few hairs shorter and coarser than those of a woman, and of more natural colour than those of the old duke. A policeman, too, in moving a table that had been upset, picked up a button bearing the arms of the Villaneras. Lastly,

the drawer in which Madame Chermidy had placed her
money was quite empty.   Hence, another assassin
must be sought than the duke.   Lump was cross-
examined, but no light could be drawn from her : she
merely struck her forehead, and said, " What a fool I
was ! That is the scoundrel ! I should like to have
him flayed alive ; but what is the good—he would
speak.   Bury my mistress, throw me ont on the dungheap, and let him go to the devil !"

The police proceeded the same day to the Villa
Dandolo, where they found Mathieu Mantoux sewing
a button on his red waistcoat.   It was noticed that
the button was new, and that his hair resembled
the specimen found in Madame Chermidy's hand.
On being arrested he exclaimed, through old associa-
tions, " little luck."   Mr. Stevens sent him to Guild-
ford Castle, on the west of the town, on the beach.
He was so fortunate as to escape during the night, but
he fell into one of those large nets which fishermen
spread at night and take up in the morning.

CHAPTER XV.

CONCLUSION.

IF you have seen the sea at the period of the equi-
noctial gales, when the yellow waves mount foaming
to the top of the pier, when the shingle mourns as the
sea beats over it, when the wind howls through the
gloomy sky, and the tide brings in scattered fragments
of wreck interlaced with seaweed—if you have seen
all this, then go and see it again in summer, and you
will not recognise the scene. The shining pebbles are
arranged side by side ou the beach, the sea is spread
out like a blue sheet beneath the smiling azure of the
sky ; the huge oxen lying on the cliff idly turn their
nostrils to the spring breeze ; white sails glisten in the
distance ; and the pink sunshades of the ladies ornament the pier.

The Count and Countess de Villanera, after a long
tour, of which Paris never knew the history, returned,
three months back, to their town mansion. The
countess dowager, who started with them, and the
Duchess de la Tour, who joined them on the old
duke's death, share without jealousy the management
of the household and the education of a beautiful child.
It is a girl, and bears a striking likeness to its mother;

hence she is more beautiful than her elder brother, the late Marquis de los Montes.

Dr. le Bris is still the physician and best friend of the family. The duke and the little marquis both died in his arms, the first at Corfu, the other at Rouen, where he caught a typhus fever.

The little marquis is said to have had a fortune of nearly a quarter million left him by a distant relation : on the death of the child, the family sold the estates and expended the money in pious works.

A chapel has been recently built to the south of the island of Corfu, on the site of the Villa Dandolo : it is served by a young priest of exemplary piety and sorrow, M. Gaston de Vitré.

THE END.

LONDON:
SAVILL, EDWARDS AND CO., PRINTERS, CHANDOS STREET,
COVENT GARDEN.

www.ingramcontent.com/pod-product-compliance
Lightning Source LLC
Chambersburg PA
CBHW031345020726
47499CB00005B/1406